DREAM MAN

"Once You Open and
Consume the Contents
Beneath This Cover,
They Will Know
Who You Are . . ."

Royce D. Williams Sr.

authorHOUSE®

AuthorHouse™
1663 Liberty Drive
Bloomington, IN 47403
www.authorhouse.com
Phone: 1 (800) 839-8640

Published by AuthorHouse 08/07/2017

ISBN: 978-1-5462-0310-0 (sc)
ISBN: 978-1-5462-0309-4 (e)

Print information available on the last page.

Any people depicted in stock imagery provided by Thinkstock are models, and such images are being used for illustrative purposes only. Certain stock imagery © Thinkstock.

This book is printed on acid-free paper.

Contents

Chapter 1 1

Chapter 2 6

Chapter 3 12

Chapter 4 16

Chapter 5 21

Chapter 6 39

Chapter 7 44

Chapter 8 52

Chapter 9 55

Chapter 10 60

Chapter 11 69

Chapter 12 72

Chapter 13 76

Chapter 14 80

Chapter 15 84

Chapter 16 91

Chapter 17 97

Chapter 18 101

Chapter 19 105

Chapter 20 109

Chapter 21 115
Chapter 22 120
Chapter 23 128
Chapter 24 132
Chapter 25 140
Chapter 26 145
Chapter 27 152
Chapter 28 163

Warning:

For those of you who open and consume
the contents beneath this cover.
They will know who you are.

For

*My two unborn children
of whom were denied Life.*

"I have never forgotten you."

CHAPTER 1

Four fifteen a.m. Friday morning, He walks across the circus grounds. As gusts of whirl winds twirl around him, he can feel the lost souls taunting him. Due to the early hour of the morning, the circus is both empty and full at the same time. He feels the impressions from happy people enjoying themselves just moments ago. He walks through the grounds in search of something. Something he's been looking for all his life. He knows that it likes the crowds. He knows, in fact that wherever people dwell it will always be there among them. Hunting for pleasure. Hunting to feed its appetite. Both are mutually exclusive to its desires. Its victims tempt it in such a way. Much like, a child in a gigantic candy store or if you like, something bloodthirsty and horrible loose in an overcrowded hen house.

He crosses a section of the circus grounds near one of the children's merry go round rides. All at once the scene of a small family confronts him. He turns and views a nearby apartment complex. By the looks of it the complex is upper to middle class. He knows that history dictates that it doesn't like low income slum housing. He thinks to himself that it will be night again soon. Paris, Italy, London, Russia and Japan it exists everywhere and nowhere at all. But now its here. Back to the country where it all began. Back to where it was born.

Later that same evening at seven twenty eight p.m. Mr. Charles P. Colvack is lying on his couch in the living room when his wife Rebecca enters the room to wake him up. She tip toes across the hard wood floors carefully not making a sound. She gets to the coffee table and grabs a cushion off the love seat. Still sound asleep she stands over her husband's limp body. She raises her arms with the cushion tightly clenched in her hands. Charles is enjoying a restful sleep. He works a full twelve hour job on the midnight shift, six days a week. He has just achieved the best posture possible on his old couch. In the past Rebecca and Charles have waged war over his favorite old couch. She and her mother, along with several girlfriends, have had their eye on a new one for quite some time. Just seeing him resting and enjoying himself in quiet peaceful slumber literally drives her insane. Maybe that's why she suddenly began to beat him repeatedly about the head and face.

Charles, now fully broken from a comfortable sleep, is responding to the assault by shouting. "What, the fuck is it!"

Rebecca responding just as loudly, "You need to go get the kids from my mothers."

Charles grabs Rebecca around the middle of her slender frame and pulls her on to him. Rebecca's options for a continuous assault are now limited. She proceeds to straddle him in an effort to win at any cost. Rebecca tries to smother Charles with the cushion but is unsuccessful when he starts to tickle her on both sides of her body. Rebecca knows that Charles is all too familiar with the fact that she can't stand to be tickled. So much in fact that once he made her lose control of her bladder during a picnic. Rebecca gives in almost immediately and Charles snatches the cushion from her hands.

He smiles and asks; "Is it time already?"

"Yep," replied Rebecca. "And it's your turn to be the man so get up and go get them."

Charles chuckles as Rebecca gets off of him. He sits up to find his shoes as she leaves the room. Charles gets his keys and heads out to pick up the kids. With Charles now gone, upstairs Rebecca prepares to take a nice soothing hot soak in the bath tub. She starts the water and runs it into the tub from the faucet. She goes back to the master bed room and gets undressed. Once she's finished disrobing she puts on Charles's robe and puts the dirty clothing in the hamper.

As she proceeds down the main hallway she breaks out into a rock n roll song. She makes her way down the hall giving it her all. Her performance was in front of a packed imaginary coliseum filled with adoring fans screaming and chanting her name. She gets to the bath room and soaks in a tub filled with bubbles, oils and different fragrances. No doubt that when Charles gets back, she'll win the battle of the couch wars before the end of the night.

Now lying back in the tub with her eyes closed and her head on an inflatable pillow, she begins to go into her return engagement at the coliseum. She starts out with something a great deal slower and a bit more romantic. Once again the place is packed and as usual she's not disappointing them. They'd go anywhere to see her. They'd come see her even if she was standing on a milk crate in the middle of Broadway Ave in down town St. Louis. They are her loyal fans and they'd stand in the pouring rain for her.

When she looks into the crowd she sees Charles and their kids. She thinks to herself that Charles looks much older since she's last seen him. It must be the stress of taking care of their children. She always told him that he'd miss her when she was gone and now that she's seen him after all these years. She could hardly recognize him in the audience with his massive hair loss, bent over broken posture, sitting in an old wheelchair and pushing himself along with that cane that she sent him on one of his birthdays that she just happened to remember that year.

As she continues to groove to the tunes her arm slips over the edge of the tube. She lets it hang there just like she has done dozens of times before. The water is steaming hot and the bubbles, oils and fragrances are beginning to do their job. She feels relaxed and loose. And all her troubles seem to float away. Something lightly strokes the top of her hand. She opens her eyes and turns to see what it is. She had seen that there's nothing there. She starts to sit back in the tub, but notices that the room is still filled with steam.

She lays back and starts to get comfortable once again and sees a face at the other end of the tub. Shocked, she jumps to her feet and leaps out of the tub. After a few moments pasts by she begins to think that she couldn't have saw what she thought she did. It all had to be in her head. She pulled the curtain out of the way and at the same time the force from the curtain caused the bubbles to shift in the water.

She straightens up and places her hands on her hips thinking that she was scared over bubbles. Still a little shaken she wasn't yet willing to get back into her comfortable bath. She decides to pull the chain and drain the tub. She takes a quick glance around the bathroom just to reaffirm that she was alone. She steps back into the tub and turns on the shower to finish her bathing ritual.

With the curtain pulled she starts to complete her task. She wants to hurry but she can't help thinking that she's being silly. She snatches the scrunchie from her hair and takes a bottle of shampoo from its place on the shelf. As she lathers up her hair she thinks that it must have been her imagination. Her eyes are closed as she rinses the shampoo from her hair. She opens them to find the shower curtain open beside her. She looks out of the shower to see who was on the other side. The steam was even thicker than before. But still not too thick that she couldn't see. The bathroom was still empty. She closed the curtain once more and proceeded to finish rinsing herself off. She keeps looking out of the shower to see what is going on. She takes a bottle of facial cleanser from the same shelf and starts to wash her face. Once she rinses her face she opens her eyes and discovers that the shower is open again but this time from the opposite end. Suddenly she figures that the prankster must be Charles trying to get even with her for having sabotaged his comfortable sleep and making him go get the kids. She says.

"You know, Charlie! You can be a real, asshole! Just, because I made you get up and go get the kids! You think it's alright to try and scare me! You know that I don't like to be afraid and at home alone. You are such a, jerk! I mean it! You just wait till I get out of here! You're going to get it! I swear you are going to, get it! Just you, wait!"

Now done she rips open the curtain and grabs the robe. Because of the thick fog like steam, she could barely see her way to the door. She feels for the door handle and snatches the door wide open. She storms into the hallway, yelling and screaming at the top of her voice. She hears her own angry voice echoing back at her. She stops yelling to see if she could hear where everyone was. She knows with Charles home the children would be watching TV in their rooms. But there was nothing, not a sound. She turns to look at the clock on the wall and quickly realizes that Charles couldn't have gotten back with the kids in such a short time.

She slowly walks back to the bathroom confused. She can't understand it, but thinking that she was just imagining it all, she walks into the bathroom. The steam is now a thick fog and the curtain has been pulled across the shower. She can't see anything at all but still she walks up to the shower itself. She can hear the water running full speed.

She starts thinking that if Charles has put something in the tub. He won't divorce him. She'll just kill him and bury his body in one of the kid's toy boxes. With the amount of toys the kids have, no one will ever find him. She rips the curtain back and a thick fog stands in its place. She fans the fog out of the way and turns off the water.

Behind her the door slams shut. She whips around so fast that she loses her footing on the wet floor. She bounces as she lands on the floor. The thick fog becomes motionless in the center of the bathroom floor. For a moment she looks into it. The thick heavy mist widens and almost reaches the ceiling. A large grin forms in the center of it and as the light switch is pulled she is consumed by darkness. Rebecca's last moments of fear are now a reality that's heard throughout the upstairs hallway. It echoes throughout the peaceful serenity of all the empty rooms of her home.

CHAPTER 2

Six seventeen A.M. Saturday morning, Suzan Timbers, a crime scene virgin just fresh out of law school and the academy is standing outside of the glass sliding doors in the rear of the Colvack's home. She's having trouble holding down a late supper from the night before. She's also just recently decided to give up on trying to maintain a strong mental, emotional and not to mention that cast iron stomach that the others seemed to have achieved.

She has only been at the crime scene a little over thirteen seconds. Ten were spent getting through all the assorted personal checking her photo identification at different points. However, after she reached the first portion of the home where Miss Colvack's body had been found baking in the oven set at 325 degrees. She never made it through the rest of the trail.

After the timeless routine of grip and release, memory lane replays the last time that she was this sick. It was pledge time back at the University and she had just made it through hell week initiations. Thinking back boy, that night is still a blur. The sun had just started to break free from a once clouded sky. She was blinded by its rays and it seemed to add to her nausea. Hearing the footsteps of another investigator and fearing even further embarrassment. She started to step off the porch but dizziness over takes her and she loses her balance. She lands in the bushes near the back of the house and her shame is complete.

Egean Shepard stands in the main hallway upstairs, just down the hall from the main bathroom. He's reading the preliminary reports of the first responding municipality patrolmen and he also reads through the first hand field notes of those who responded from his office.

Angry, he lets out a wail. "Jeff! Where the hell are you?"

Jeff Henderson rushes up from the stairs screaming, "Yes sir."

"Where the hell is he?" Egean asks.

Jeff, while examining the polish on his shoes, shrugs his shoulders and says. "I don't know."

Egean picks up on Jeff's caviler attitude in his response and says. "Look, I don't give a damn if you guys don't get along. I'm asking you where is he?"

Jeff, knows that Egean is angry and in no mood for any bad behavior on his part. He responds to the question in a low and calm voice. "Sir, I don't know where he is and I did call his cell, his home number and I even paged him. He hasn't bothered to call me back."

Egean just takes a deep breath and says. "There's going to be some changes around here. Real soon and that's a promise."

Jeff exhibits some foresight and doesn't give Egean any feedback. The two are joined by Timbers and she gives Jeff her paper work on the team's findings down stairs.

Jeff takes a glance at the info and says. "Where's the rest of the report?"

Timbers replies; "Sir, That's all they gave me down there."

Jeff shoves the paper work back into her hands and says. "Look, take this and go back and get the rest of it. Don't you ever do this again."

Puzzled, Timbers says; "Sir, what did I do?"

Jeff looks at her and sharply answers. "First, you're new so you haven't earned any points that allow you the privilege of being late to a crime scene. Second, instead of being here and prepared, you're running around trying to play catch up and you can't even get the paper work right."

She starts to take the paper work and leave. But before she can Jeff sees her and sharply speaks again. "Now where are you going?"

She turns and answers him. "Sir, you just told me that my paper work is incomplete. I am going back down stairs to complete it."

Jeff says; "What I also wanted is for you guys to work your way from the beginning of the house downstairs and finish up with the upstairs. Do you even know why I want this?"

Timbers shakes her head no. Jeff explains, "The reason that I want you guys to work your way up from downstairs is because usually you can tell where the victim was first accosted in the home. Now, where is the first sign of attack?"

Timbers is now agitated, but is careful not to say a word. She shakes her head and wishes that this morning's lecture was over. But she knows that she stood a better chance of lightning striking her dead than Jeff. The acid was now starting to rebuild itself at an incredible rate. She could feel the inside lining of her stomach beginning to burn.

Jeff sees that she is not mentally engaged in obtaining the benefit of his vast years of experiences so he tasks her again by saying. "Perhaps you can tell me where the victim first encountered her attacker?"

Timbers replies; "I don't know where she was first approached. I would have to see the entire house to make that determination, Sir."

Jeff replies, "You mean, you haven't seen the whole house yet?"

"No." Timbers replies.

Jeff now even angrier than before looks to see where Egean has been during his conversation with Timbers. He sees that Egean has been talking on his cell phone.

"Come here!" Jeff says in a low voice.

He leads her down the hallway towards the main bathroom. He stops just short and says. "Look at these walls. Tell me what you see."

Timbers takes a moment to examine the wall and says, "Its blood put into some kind of pattern."

Jeff says. "What kind of pattern? I mean are they circles, triangles, squares or are they shapes of apples or oranges? I need you to be specific."

Timbers seems lost for a comment. She can't really put it into words. At first it didn't seem like anything other than just large splashes of blood on the wall. The killer must have used a bucket to cover so much space. The entire walls on both sides of the hallway were covered. It was something that must have taken a long time to do. She knows that a great deal of the house had been covered in blood. Some of the down stairs rooms had almost no blood in them at all. Some rooms weren't even touched, whereas some rooms like the mess in the kitchen turned her inside out. Mentally recapping the events that led to her lying in the bushes in the rear of the house, she began to feel her stomach return to its rotation of grip and release once again. She started to back into Jeff. He sees her starting to lose it and takes the opportunity to do what he calls toughening her up. He puts out his hands and stops her from backing up.

Timbers, grabs her stomach and tells him. "I have to go."

Jeff again stops her and says; "Look, either you have a taste for this work or you don't."

Knowing that she is about to lose her dinner again. She can't decide which is worse. The embarrassments that'll come from her losing it in front of Jeff, who undoubtedly will never let her, live it down. She just realized that Jeff and the others are on to her losing it out back. The pain and the shame together with the impending erupting force inside of her are more than she can handle.

She thinks to herself that she knows she can't lose it here. Not in the house, everything will be contaminated. That's rule number one of crime scene investigations. Her professor, if he were ever to find out, would probably never talk to her again. She tries to still get around Jeff. But he still taunts her, not letting her get by. Not letting her freely pass by him at all.

She can't take it any longer and runs into the nearby bathroom. As she enters the bathroom she slips on a large amount of blood and lands on the back of her head followed by her back. The rest of her body slams into the tiles on the bathroom floor and her face is immediately covered with a cold wet bath towel. She feels herself being turned over. She releases herself into the towel and props her elbow under her body. Taking the towel from around her face and wiping it on a clean portion.

She looks up at him, kneeling beside her on one knee. He doesn't speak a word to her. She sees behind him deep dark traces of blood on the walls of the bathroom. As she starts to look around the bathroom the thick and heavy smeared shapes in black blood, human tissue and bone fragments scream out to her. She realizes that she is there. She's in the place where the victim was first accosted by the killer. The two are joined by Egean and Jeff.

Egean says. "Where the hell have you been?"

He doesn't say a word. Instead he looks down at her and says. "Do you want to stand up?"

She gets to her knees and wraps the soiled bath towel. She stands and walks past Jeff saying. "You're an asshole."

Egean looks at Jeff and says. "What's she talking about?"

As Jeff watched Timbers clear the hallway he answers Egean with shrugged shoulders.

"You know, lately that seems to be your answer for everything." Said Egean. He then turned his attention back to his first question and said; "Where have you been? I hear that Jeff called and paged you."

He stood up and without a word, walked past the two men. Egean called out to him. "Sebastian, stop for a moment."

Sebastian stops as Egean and Jeff approach him. Jeff says. "How did you get by us?"

Sebastian doesn't say a word.

Jeff gets angry and charges Sebastian saying. "Did you hear me?"

Sebastian doesn't move an inch and this in turn changes Jeff's body language from one of a confident assault to a timid soft whisper.

Jeff says again. "Man, if you don't want to work with me. Just tell Egean so I don't look like an ass calling around for your ass."

Sebastian replies in a low calm voice. "Jeffrey, the next time you call yourself attempting to scare me. I advise you to pack a sack lunch because it's going to take you a long time."

Jeff started to respond to him but Egean cut him off by saying. "O.K., that's enough. Jeff go make sure that your so called paper work is in order down stairs."

Jeff looked at him with a surprised look on his face. Egean said. "Yeah, you thought that I wasn't paying attention."

Jeff walks down the hallway and disappears as he goes down the stairs. Egean looks back at Sebastian. Sebastian's face goes blank as he starts to study the walls of the hallway.

Egean says. "Well?"

Sebastian answers. "Well, what?"

Egean says; "Well, what do you think of this mess? He really out did himself this time. Don't ya think?"

Sebastian continued to look over the walls and not say word. He looked passed Egean like he wasn't even there. It was like he was replaying the events in his mind.

Egean said; "The husband was supposed to be out picking up the kids. At first we did think that it was him but we found out that he had a flat tire after he left to get the kids. The Auto Club had to drive out and meet up with him to change the tire. He didn't get back until late last night. When he got back the door was open, the kitchen was filled with smoke and the fire alarm was going off. So far we think that the reason he put her in the kitchen oven and started her to cook at such a high temperature was so she would be discovered by her neighbors before her husband got back. The husband is at the hospital, his kids are back over at the grandparents."

Egean looked at Sebastian, who was lost in thought. Egean says; "Have you heard from her?"

Sebastian looked at Egean and said nothing.

Egean said. "You know, everybody talks to me but you. Now why is that? Do you suppose that maybe it's because, in addition to my years with the F.B.I. Behavioral Crime Units. I also served as a counselor to several of, in my personal opinion, the best F.B.I. Profilers and Investigators in these United States. Also, not to mention my work with the Military combat Veterans. Who knows, if you're going to talk to me. Maybe you'll get better at dealing with this thing that you've been going through. I don't know, maybe you'll feel better. I mean, after all. What has it been, at least ten years?"

Sebastian completed his examination of some stains on the floor. He stood up and turned and proceeded to walk down the hallway and out of the house.

Egean, still wanting to be heard, says to himself; "Sooner or later you got to talk to someone."

CHAPTER 3

The moon is full of light. Its rays illuminate the night in such a way, that if not for the clear view of the night's stars, one would think it were day time. For centuries these rays have been the cause of all things strange, eerie, sinister and passionate that occur between the dusk till dawn.

He splashes the thick blue paint like substance on to his brushes. He lies upon her, stretching her upper torso over the back of the couch. She's naked and totally exposed to his generous expressions of tender eroticism, as well as his explosions of horrific sadistic torture. He enters her from behind again and again. The fire is so great that the flames ignite within her a scream that shatters the top of her voice. During the writhing of each climactic moment of pleasure and pain.

The two are joined by a third. Though he's not a participant, he can't help but be drawn to what was taking place. The room is filled with the glow of the moons illuminating light. He looks around the room and sees the clean spots where pictures hung in frames that now lay at the bottom of the walls themselves. He looks upon a room of flipped over furniture and broken glass from vases and glasses that once occupied the tables of the room. He turns to see the makings of a painting on the wall behind him. It resembles someone that he's seen before. He tries to remember who. He studies her face as much as he can, but there's not enough of the painting there to aid him in figuring out just who it is.

Slam! The body of the naked woman strikes the wall of the partial painting that the young boy stood looking at. She falls to the floor beneath the painting and lands at his feet. He turns to look for him, the man who causes great pain and delight simultaneously. He's not there. The young boy still visually searching the room for him. The moon light, now starting to dim. Suddenly the couch is thrown across the room. The young boy looks to see what threw the couch, but there was nothing there. As though it was clearing things out of its path. First a chair then a table and finally another table. Clearing a path directly towards him. At his feet screams are heard. The young boy looks down at her.

She grabs hold of the young boy's leg and screams; "Oh God, not again! This time he's going to kill me!"

The young boy reaches for the woman but she is snatched from the young boy's leg. Kicking and screaming, she digs her nails into the floor, trying to avoid the inedible. As her body is dragged alongside the baseboard of the wall.

She pleads with the young boy for her life. "Help me! Help me please!"

She's dragged around the corner and into the hallway. Her hands catch hold of the corner of the wall as she fights for one last chance at life. Still screaming, her hands continuing to hold on to the corner of the wall. The young boy jumps for the woman's hands. He grabs the hands of the woman and she responds by gripping his hands as tight as she can. The grip of her right hand starts to loosen in his. He tries to tighten his grip, but he loses her right hand all at once. Fearing that he might lose her all together, he grabs hold of her left hand with both of his hands. Tighter and tighter he holds on, but he could feel the powerful strength of the one at the opposite end of her. The young boy couldn't help but feel that he must have been responsible for the woman's body being thrown across the room and the couch as well. The young boy started thinking that with that kind of strength; he had to be toying with the both of them. He started to wonder why he was playing with us. Why bother to take so long. Why not just take what you want.

Suddenly her hand went limp in his. He got to his knees and crawled up the corner of the wall. The hallway was pitch black and as the young boy stood up. He looked down at his hand and saw that he was still holding the left hand of the naked woman. The end had been torn out and the ragged part was dripping. He started to examine the hand and pull its grip free from his hand. Once free, a scream is heard from the hallway and the hand reacts and yanks itself free from the young boy's hand and latches on to the young boy's neck.

"Wake up! Wake up! Wake up now, Danny!" He wakes up and sees his mother leaning over him and yelling.

He sprang out of bed and raced passed her. Once out of his bed room, he makes it through the hallway and into the bathroom. He shuts the door and runs into the shower. He turns on the cold water and sits on the floor. His mother gets to the door and begins knocking. She starts trying to open the door and after a few twists she discovers that it is locked.

She starts knocking and saying; "Danny! Danny! Please open the door! Danny, can you hear me? Danny, please open the door!"

The cold water running through his hair and down his face, chest and back seemed soothing. He couldn't help but think about the whole thing over and over. The hand that gripped his. The partial paintings on the walls. He still can't remember who she was. He really doesn't want to think about it anymore. He thought that these thoughts weren't supposed to come back any more. Listening to the concern in his mother's voice. Danny starts thinking that she's going to worry if the dreams are back. Danny starts thinking that if he doesn't answer her soon, she might call the psychiatrist. He didn't want her to have to spend any more money on anymore shrinks. He didn't want her to spend anymore nights worrying about him and watching over him sleep. He just can't put her through it. Not again, not after all that she's been through already. The cold water has done its job and he begins to feel better. His mother continues is beating on the door.

Danny snatches it open and says. "Mom, I got to take a shower or else I'll be late for work."

He closes the door and takes a shower. Fifteen minutes later, he springs out of the bathroom and runs back into his bedroom. Twenty minutes later, Danny bolts from his bedroom and as he runs out of the hallway and into the living room his mother burst into laughter from looking at Danny's restaurant uniform. She laughed even harder when he turned around and looked at her sitting at the kitchen table.

Now armed with the full view she stops laughing enough to say. "Tell me what are you supposed to be?"

Danny replies; "I'm a chip monk. At least that's what I think I'm supposed to be."

His mother said; "If you wanted money why didn't you just ask me? When did you get this job?"

Danny replies; "Mom, I wanted to earn my own money this time. I just got this job the other day. After all, we talked about me getting a job."

"I know, where's this place at?" She asked.

"It's just past Oceans Dr. on the hill." Danny answered. He went on to say. "Mom, I have to go. I'll be late for my first day."

His mother proudly says; "O.k. O.k. You'd better get going then. Next time you want money just ask for it. O.k.?"

Danny says. "O.k. Mom."

He puts on his hat and the entire ensemble is so funny. His mother bursts into laughter once again. Danny shakes his head and turns and runs to out of the house.

CHAPTER 4

Eight forty eight p.m. Thursday evening, at a local University. The halls echo with the sounds of her shoes on a linoleum floor. Helen Saunders is tired of cooking class. Her steps do not go unheard. She has a eerie feeling that someone is following her. She tries not to give away her thoughts. She doesn't know what he will do if he senses that she is on to him.

The University is all but closed and everyone is either gone or in the process of going home. Suddenly she stops at a hallway. Its silent dark walls seem to call out to her. It whispers to her that it has a secret to tell. She stops at the entrance to it and stares down the long hollow hallway. She can see a white row of tiles on both sides of the beginning of the hall. She visually follows both of them as they disappear into the darkness towards the end of the hall.

Helen is well known for her curiosity. In fact there are some who would say that her nosy streak is legendary to those who know her personally. Finally her human nature gets the better of her and before she knows it, she has already taken the plunge. At first she steps lightly and slowly. The anticipation is so great, she can taste it on her lips. Like a moth to a flame, she passes door after door. Her pace is, much louder and much faster now.

The light from the moon shines through the windows of each class room. Its beaming presence breaks through and lands in the hallway. She stops at a door, not just any door mind you; but the door that serves as the entrance to a horrifying tale. She tries to see inside the blackened classroom. It's difficult, all so difficult but she doesn't want to give up.

Especially since she's come so far. She almost lost her nerve several times over and over, just coming down the hall. She tries her luck and turns the door knob. At first It seems to be locked. She shakes the knob and like magic it slowly opens and she can't believe her luck or lack of it. As she enters the class room, she can feel a sense of eeriness fall over her. There were holes in the walls and a strange smell that at first you didn't notice when you entered the room. But like a trap, it had you once you were in its embrace. Steam began to fall from her lips as the temperature of the room suddenly plummeted.

"What the hell are you doing in there?!" The voice came from a face that peered at her through a crack in the wall.

She immediately started looking for another way out of the classroom but all that she could see was nothing but darkened walls. Not wanting to accept that she was stuck with no way to escape. She looked back at the crack and the face was gone. She started looking again for a way out. Hoping for another door, she starts walking towards the opposite end of the classroom. She starts bumping into furniture in the thick blackness. The lights are turned on and she is blinded for a moment.

The same voice said. "What the hell are you doing in here?"

Still attempting to focus she answered; "I was lost and I couldn't find my way out."

"No, you didn't find this classroom by accident. You were looking for it." He replied.

Now able to focus she replies; "Why, what's so important about this room?"

He said. "Don't act as though you don't know about this room. Everybody knows about this room."

She looked around her and realized that she was at the end of the classroom. She was hoping for a way out, but there was no other door. The furniture was piled high in the corner to her left. She could see a sort of tarp that hung across the wall with nails behind the stacks of furniture.

She asked. "Hey, what's that?"

He said. "I knew that you were one of those guys. One of those sickos."

"I don't know what you're talking about. I was lost, so I came in here to look out of the window to see where the parking lot was. I figured that it was a good way to see where I was." She replied.

He looked at her for a moment. It was like he was trying to figure from look on her face if she was lying or not.

Finally he said; "The parking lot is at the opposite end of the campus. Come on out and I'll show you where it is."

She said; "Who are you?"

"My name is Todd Glowczwski. I'm the night janitor on this side of the campus." He answered.

She started to come out but snagged her sweater on some of the furniture. She tried to get it unsnagged. But it just wouldn't come off.

He sees that she is having trouble and says; "Stop, because you're going to tear it. Here, let me help you."

He started pushing tables out of the way as he came towards her, she started examining him more closely. He was kind of chubby, but he didn't seem to have any trouble with the job at hand. Since they had been engaged in conversation, she was a little more at ease. But still there was something odd about him. Something she couldn't quite put her finger on. He reached around her waist with his bare like hairy arm and unhooked her garment. She slipped by him and backed up to the center of the room.

She stood there getting a wider view of the area of the wall where the tarp was located. He looked at her and at first didn't say a word. She studied the room from side to side. The floor had recently under gone some tiling. In fact, the whole room seemed to be under reconstruction. Some areas were covered in dust and there was thick, heavy, black, mud looking stuff all over the place. There was a trail of it that zig zagged on the floor. There was a lot of it in some spots. It looked as if it had been poured throughout the room. During the time she took studying the class room. It occurred to her that he was still there, quietly waiting.

"What happened in here?" She asked.

Staring at the floor he said. "No one really knows. It was just something bad that happened."

She said. "What's all that black stuff? Is it tar?"

"The University still doesn't want us to talk about it. Some people have lost their jobs already." He replied.

She said. "But this stuff all looks like it happened a long time ago."

He said. "Yeah, it was a very long time ago. The University was never going to use this room again. It's been lock away and the doors and windows bolted. Until recent it didn't even have a room number. It was never supposed to be used again."

"Why is it being used now? I mean, it looks like they're getting ready to start using it again. Am I right?" She asked.

"Yes." He answered. He continued on to say; "We have a new committee and a new Dean of students. His name is Arthur T. Kimbrel and he doesn't care about the reputation of this room. He doesn't care about what happened here. He's basically a money man. The old Dean, Dean Alexander H. Venetis kept this classroom sealed".

"Why did he do that?" She asked.

"Well, after all that happened here. Dean Venetis believed that this place needed to be forgotten. It was he who pushed the committee to close and bolt its doors, zero out its classroom number and conceal its existence. He felt that he didn't want the University to carry the awful reputation of that day. So he did all that he could to put the publicity of the events of what happened in here behind it."

"So, why reopen it now?" She asked.

He replies; "That's Dean Kimbrel's doing. He doesn't care about anything that Dean Venetis or the old committee cared about. He'd rather do away with the old University traditions of honor, respect and integrity. He wants to ruin this place. He always has. There are people who have worked their entire lives here. Their children have graduated here and their kids, kids are still graduating here. Kimbrel's going to change all of that. Just as fast as he can."

She started looking around the room again and saw that several of the windows were broken. Not wanting him to usher her towards the door too soon she asked. "Sounds like you don't have too much love for this guy."

"Well there's a history there. Turns out I know him well." He replies.

She starts staring at the tarp on the back wall of the classroom again and feeling more comfortable with him. She walks right past him and asks. "Why's that?"

Trying to figure out what could be behind the tarp on the wall was killing her sense of curiosity. Those who have seen her in action in her past, know all too well that this was not a good thing. Not at all. Some would consider it dangerous. Something got her attention. It was the quietness. He had stopped talking. Spooked, from the sudden rush of mental possibilities. She quickly swung her body around and found him staring at a hole in the floor.

She said; "What's that?"

Looking at the hole in the floor, he replied; "It was bad."

"What was bad?" She asked.

"That day." He answered.

She stood still in suspended animation. Her nose for curiosity was in full swing. It could tell that what she had been waiting for was finally about to reveal itself...

CHAPTER 5

Danny was cleaning the main dining room of The Happy Chip Monk Miracle World restaurant. He wiped off all of the tables and set the chairs on top of them. He already had a bucket of hot soapy water ready and waiting for mopping. After he had completed mopping the floor. He took out the trash and started wiping down the counters in the back near the grill.

"Hey, what are you trying to do, kid?" Mr. Lesko said, while standing over Danny's shoulder.

Danny stopped wiping the counter and turned to give Mr. Lesko a look of surprise. "Am I doing something wrong?" He replied.

"No, I just want these other guys to do their fair share. That's all." Answered, Mr. Lesko. He went on to say. "You're doing great and don't let anyone tell you any different. O.k.?"

Danny nodded his head yes and continued working. Later, after his shift was done for the day, Danny stopped for gas on his way home. He went into Madelyn's, it was a Convenient Mart and gas station. He found himself waiting in a long line. As he neared the counter, he expected to see the same cashier as always. Usually, it would be this girl he knew from High school. Her name was Darla Kavanaugh and he'd known her since her family moved here to the city of Soft Stone Cove California from New York, when he was in the second grade. At the time she and he had a lot in common, seeing as how he had just moved here himself from St. Louis Missouri. They weren't the best of friends mind you, but they were still kind of friends. After a moment or two had passed, Danny was now third in line. Once the large heavy set biker, who had been impatiently waiting for his turn made it to the counter, he slammed a case of beer down on the counter.

He said; "Why's it taking so long for you to do your job? People have got better things to do than to stand around here, waiting on you to get better at your job. You should learn how to do your job on a much slower shift. Like a earlier shift when not so many people are off from work and trying to gas up their cars and their guts.

A female voice jumped back at him saying; "Hey, well from what I can tell. People around here gas their car's and their guts twenty four hours a day. So, when do you really suggest that I learn how to do my job?"

Immediately, Danny realized that the female voice behind the counter wasn't Darla's. Even though he didn't mind waiting for his turn, he thought it was kind of taking longer than usual for Darla to clear the customers out of the store. After all she'd been working here since two summers ago. He tried to look around the big Biker, with his tattoos that out lined an entire life time of hard living, inscribed up and down both of his arms. His shoulders were too broad for Danny to see the cashier, who was now dealing with the Biker on his level.

The Biker responded with; "I was just trying to give you some advice on how not to piss people off. After all it seems like you need it."

The voice responded in return; "O, I'm sorry sir. I misunderstood. I thought you were trying to make the transition of me learning how to do my job harder than it had to be. When, here all along, you were just trying to help me. I was so far off, the mark. You know, I owe you an apology. I am, so sorry sir. Please forgive me."

The Biker answered; "That's O.k."

She finished ringing up his order and as he walked towards the exit with his beer and change. She said. "Thank you, sir. Drive carefully and please come again."

"Yeah, right." The Biker replied with a grunt.

Finally, Danny could see the girl behind the counter. He recognized her because in a small southern town like Soft Stone Cove, everyone knows when you're a new face. He'd always thought that she was beautiful. But he was always too shy around girls to approach any of them in more than just a friendly way. But Danny, thought she was more attractive than any one he'd seen in his life ever. So attractive in fact that he didn't realize the last guy ahead of him had already left the counter and exited the store.

A fact that became clear to everyone in the store when she asked. "Did you have any gas? I said, did you have any gas? Are you alright?"

Danny snapped out of the trance of her beauty. Shocked and embarrassed he quickly closes the gap between the counter and himself.

Now face to face with her, he swallows and says; "I'm sorry. I was just thinking about something."

She smiles and says; "That's o.k. It's only when people don't take the time to think that the really big problems in life start to occur."

He appreciated her letting him off the hook, so he could still approach the counter and pay for his gas. Afterwards, he walked towards the exit, afraid to look back fearing that if by some slim chance. It wasn't obvious to her and everyone else before, that he found her attractive. A last glance might tip them off at that point or seal any conclusions that they may have.

Danny drove down Clairmore St. he noticed a house with smoke escaping from the side of a window. He stopped in front of the house and got out. He looked at the front door and could see smoke coming from every corner of it. He tried the door knob, but he wasn't at all surprised at the fact that it was locked. He quickly hurried around to the back door. As he past by the side windows of the home, he could see that all of them were closed with smoke clearly seeping from their sides. He reached the back door of the house and twisted the door knob. The door opened wide and a large amount of smoke forced him back down the steps of the porch. The smoke let up a moment and Danny covered his eyes and went in. It was impossible to see. He reached his hands out everywhere to feel his way. Although the smoke was heavy throughout the rooms, he had a sense of where he was going. He went through the hall and looked into the kitchen, but there was nothing cooking. Even though it was hard to tell, he could still detect that the smoke was coming from the front of the house. He continued down the hallway until he came to what seemed like the entrance to the main room of the home.

Flashes of his most recent dream started to surface. The long hallway had started to bring it all back. The smoke was much like the darkness of the night. From the hall he could hear a tremendous sizzling sound. His most recent dream still haunting his thoughts, he stepped into what probably was the living room. In the center of the room, he could make out the figure of a man struggling. He came closer to try and get a better look. Once he was beside the man, he took a look at what the Smokey figure was struggling with. It was a large slab of ribs on top of an enormous grill.

Danny looked over at the man beside him and said. "Uncle Aaron, what the hell are you doing?"

Uncle Aaron looked over and discovered his nephew standing beside him and replied; "Hell Danny, where did you come from?"

Danny said; "Can we open a window?"

Uncle Aaron thought for a moment and realized that his nephew may not be able to breathe. The two of them started opening windows all around the living room and when enough windows were opened they went outside for some fresh air.

Sitting on the porch Danny asked. "Uncle Aaron are you trying to kill yourself?"

Uncle Aaron looked at Danny and replied; "Did your mother send you over here to ask me that?"

"No, no no. That's just something that I'm concerned about. Mom would never had sent me over here to spy on you."

Uncle Aaron stood on the porch and started thinking to himself for a moment and said; "Yeah, you're right. If she thought something like that, she'd just come and investigate for herself. Yeah, she got that from your Dad."

Hurt by Uncle Aaron's remark, Danny takes a seat on the steps of the porch. Uncle Aaron stops thinking about himself for a moment when he realizes that Danny's silence was unusual. He sits down beside him and waits for a moment.

Finally, Uncle Aaron says; "Danny, I'm sorry. I didn't mean to say anything to hurt your feelings. You know I'd never do that. Not for anything in the world."

"I know, Uncle Aaron. I know. It's o.k. I just wish that I had the chance to get to know him. I wish I could even remember what he looked like. I don't remember what the fight between him and Mom was about." Replied Danny.

Uncle Aaron, realizing that Danny was needing answers to questions that he had no way to answer, said. "Danny, you've been thinking of your father more and more, lately. You know, you're Mom, when she came home with you asked me to help her, when the day came, when you started asking questions about your Dad. She and I both knew that this day would come."

Danny looked at Uncle Aaron and said. "I'm not thinking of him. I'm just curious about a few things. That's all."

Uncle Aaron put his arm across Danny's shoulders to reassure him and said; "Danny, its o.k. if you want to know about your Dad. It's nothing that you should feel uncomfortable about. After all, your just as deserving and you have the same rights as anyone else."

Danny still trying to throw his Uncle Aaron off his trail said; "I was just a little curious, that's all."

Uncle Aaron saw through Danny's persistent attempt not to alarm him and said. "Stop it. Didn't I tell you that it was o.k. for you to ask questions about your dad? But I hate to say this. There's only two people in this whole world who are the only authority on your dad. And like it or not, one's your mother."

"Who's the other one?" Danny asked.

"The one who made us all and that's the good Lord himself." Answered Uncle Aaron.

"How'd they meet?" Danny asked.

Uncle Aaron took a deep breath and tried his best to answer. "They meet when your mom was in a lot of trouble. She had arrived in St. Louis Missouri to attend college at a huge University. She didn't want to go to the local University. She felt that it was better to get out of town and experience the aspect of living in a major city. Our parents said that she was just suffering from the small town girl thing. But they didn't try and stop her. Our parents always supported us on everything that we did, just like my sister does with you. Anyway, there she was going to classes working and just existing in the major city of St. Louis. She had always liked politics so she went into it full force there. She worked on building contacts all over Missouri, Illinois and whenever possible she even improved her contacts with other major big cities as well. She even created contacts with foreign countries."

"One time, while living at the dorm, she had a roommate. It was this girl who was also from a small town, except she was from some state like Idaho or Iowa or something like that. Anyway, your mom being the person that she is kinda took care of the girl. She showed Penny, that was the girl's name, all around and helped her get a job. She even told Penny what places to stay away from. Everything was fine for a while. Then one day, your mother got a call from another friend by the name of Emily. Emily was the girl who your mother got to give Penny a job. Emily told your mother that Penny was fine at first but lately she has changed. Emily told your mother that Penny first started by coming in late and now she hardly comes to work at all. Emily also said that when Penny did come to work, she had gotten to the point that she really wouldn't do anything at all and she was always tired. Emily told your mother that she had even discovered her sleeping a few times."

"Your mother hadn't seen Penny in awhile and one day your saw Penny being chewed out by a professor. He was upset with her for missing class, not turning in assignments and sleeping in class, his class. After the scene was over, your mother asked Penny if she was o.k. Penny became angry and told your mom to mind her own business. Well then they had words that day and your mom didn't see Penny for weeks."

"Well one afternoon, your mom gets called to the main office. Apparently, Penny hadn't been calling her folks back home and now they were worried. Penny's guidance counselor tells your mom that Penny's mother has really been franticly worried about Penny. She hasn't called in a very long time and the last time that she spoke to Penny, she got a bad feeling that Penny was in some kind of trouble. Her mother said that she tried as hard as she could, but Penny just wouldn't give in and confide in her. The guidance counselor told your mother that Penny and her mother must be very close. Penny's mother had been calling her over and over, asking her to try and help Penny."

Danny listened to his Uncle Aaron's voice as it changed. He picked up on its subtle differences as Uncle Aaron's words transported him into a mental pictured image that began to form in Danny's mind.

He went on to say that a few days later, it was about two A.M. in the morning when Penny suddenly showed up. Your mom heard her from her own bedroom. She could have stayed in bed and just said nothing, but she got to thinking about Penny's mother, worrying endlessly. After all, our own mother had your mom calling home almost every night. Now, our mother was worried about your mom to but, if my sister wasn't calling home as often as she did. Well then she would cause our mother to worry more. When she came out of her room, she found Penny packing some clothing and crying in the dark.

Your mom asked. "Are you alright?"

In spite of her being obviously upset, she answered. "Fine, I'm fine."

They stood there in the dark for a moment until your mom tried to turn on the bedroom light. Something grabbed her and held her against the wall. She said that Penny started pleading with someone to let your mother go. Penny kept telling, whoever it was that your mother couldn't come with them.

Making excuses, Penny told him. "She's got finals all this week!"

He motioned to Penny to leave the room and when she did, he whispered something scary in her ear saying. "It would be wise to forget that we were ever here. If you don't we will be back to take you with us."

Now your mom told us that it was dark in Penny's bedroom and all she could make out was he had a slender build. He seemed to be in his twenties or thirties. He was very, very strong and his voice was unusually deep.

She also told me that Penny and the stranger left the dorm room and when she left Penny's room. She went back to her own bedroom and sat on her bed, trying to figure out what she should do. She decided to call the police and she did. She talked to a Detective and he told her that he would call the night Detective.

While she was waiting for some guy to call her back, she couldn't get over how afraid Penny was. How creepy the guy was who grabbed her. While sitting on the edge of the bed, she patently waited. Her room was dark and it seemed like it was taking forever for someone to get back to her. She told us that she knew that her bedroom was empty when she got back to it. She said that behind her, in the far end of the room near the bed, she heard the sound of a cigarette lighter. She turned and stood at the same time. The cigarette burned brightly as he took a long drag on it. In the brightness of its glow, he had a smile on his face that struck fear in her. She bolted towards the door, but he was on her so fast she didn't even make it past the bedroom door. He covered her head with something and then she couldn't breathe. She past out after that.

She woke to find herself in darkness. Trying to breathe she started moving her head around. She couldn't see, her eyes lids were like lead weights. She tried and she tried, but she couldn't lift them. She told us she could feel cloth around her ears and the rest of her face, so she knew that she had a hood over her head.

That's when she heard a woman's heavy breathing. She heard strange sounds of someone struggling and a sort of sucking. She was blind and afraid. Her arms, legs and the rest of her body were still too heavy. The sounds were near her and they seemed to be getting louder. A burst of screams shattered the inside of her mind, she recognized that it was Penny. She struggled to get up, but she just couldn't. Penny was screaming so loud that your mother's eardrums were vibrating from the high pitch of her tone.

Your Mom started to cry, she thought her life was over. She squinted her eyes as tight as she could and started to pray. She cried and cried. The cover was snatched off her head and the cool air hit her in the face. She still couldn't open her eyes. She still couldn't see a thing. She was frightened to death.

The same strange heavy voice that spoke to her before, in Penny's bedroom, said. "Be calm. Let me open your eyes to something unique. Something wonderful is coming and I want you to be a part of it. I want you to share in its pleasure, but first she had to earn your right to it."

He started to take off one of the patches, as he whispered softly to her. "I loved you."

The patches were stuck to her eye lids with some kind of adhesive.

He pulled them off slowly one at a time, while continuing to whisper. "This is going to be something beautiful."

When she opened her eyes she could hardly focus. Everything was fuzzy and then blurry. He said. "You'll be able to see in a moment."

As she started to focus he began wiping her face with a wet towel. Once she was able to see clearly, he backed away slowly revealing her surroundings. The room was dark and quiet. She started looking for Penny. Before, her shrieking voice sounded like she was right in front her. She couldn't see anything, but the silence of the darkness. Even the one who was wiping her face a moment ago, seemed to disappear. Before she couldn't see anything and the world to her was terrifying. Now that she could see, she was more afraid then ever before. She tried moving her head but the restraints were constricting her movements.

"There's nothing to worry about. Are you uncomfortable?" A voice behind her said.

Out of fear, she didn't reply.

"There's nothing to be afraid of. Are you hungry?" He asked.

She could hear him moving around behind her and now there was an odor.

"The rules are simply." He said.

He continued on to say. "Well, you'd better know them or else there's going to be a lot of uncomfortable moments in your immediate future.

Rule #1. In order for this to work, you have to give of yourself freely and totally.

Rule #2. We are a work in progress and the work will be respected.

Rule #3. No matter what happens, you must remember to keep the work beautiful. Because the work is important and you are not.

Rule #4. The moment you think that you're more important than the work. You will cease to exist.

He said; "Now, are there any questions?"

Sure of himself, he stated as he walked away. "None, good."

"Where's my friend?" She asked.

The sound of his footsteps come to a halt. Surprised he says. "All this time you haven't uttered a word and now when you finally decide to open your mouth. You ask about your roommate. That's very interesting. Why ask about her?"

"She's my friend and I want to know where she is." Her words were crumbling, but sturdy. The pressure was so high, she wanted to scream at the top of her voice. The only reason she didn't was due to the fear that she thought it would be like putting blood in the water.

"She doesn't even like you. She hates your little, goody two shoes guts!" He said.

She jumped when he spoke. His voice right next to her ear. It was like he came from nowhere. She didn't hear his steps. She started thinking, maybe she was wrong. Maybe she just didn't hear him walk back to her or maybe he's been there all the time. There's no way for her to tell.

"You're new here, but don't expect that to give you any mercy. The next time you are asked a question and you fail to answer. It will prove to be a most unpleasant experience. Now, why do you care about what happens to her?" He asked again.

Both nervous and scared, she fumbles over the answer. All at once she starts to feel a small but steady piercing feeling in the small of her back. Thinking it must be from her body sitting so long in the chair, she doesn't pay too much attention to it. At first she thought she could take it, but the feeling seemed to grow into a ball of fire. The intensity was great; she started thinking that it was coming through her belly. She wanted to scream, but something was wrong. The muscles of her jaw wouldn't allow her to open her mouth. Her body started to tremble at first and then she began to shake uncontrollably. All at once her body stopped. The feeling had left as quickly as it came. Her breathing was erratic and she didn't think that she would be able to get it under control. Her face was now covered in sweat. She kept trying to figure out what just happened to her but she couldn't understand it. It was like nothing she had ever experienced in her life.

"Now, do you want to answer the question?" He asked again.

Fearing a repeat of the last experience, she replied in a strong voice. "I don't care! She's got family! I've got family! People will be looking for us! So, I'll ask you again! Where's my friend?!"

All was quiet for a moment. She waited, expecting the worse. Bracing herself for whatever happened to happen again. She still couldn't figure out just what happened before. The sensation was too unknown to her. Too, unreal.

From the same distance as before and again without the sound of even one foot step. He answered. "She's nearly finished and you should be so lucky."

Just then there was a knock at the door. She heard the loud slam of a door. A stranger was greeted at the door downstairs by Miss Pearl.

"Good evening maam, I was wondering if you could help me?" The stranger asked as he stood in the doorway.

Miss Pearl, being a very large elderly woman, wobbled as she stood in the doorway. She seemed tired and incoherent. She had dark circles under her eyes and she squinted as she tried to focus on him.

"What can I do you fer?" She asked, in a small winning voice.

He said; "Yes, maam. You can tell me, why?"

"Why what?" She asked.

"Why do you have blood all over your upstairs walls." He answered.

She smiled and said; "Come on in. We've been waiting for you, my son."

He stepped over the threshold and walked in. She closed the door behind him and when he turned to look at her, she wasn't there anymore. He looked up to the ceiling and like a large cat; she landed on him, knocking him to the floor. She gripped him. Her arms felt like they were made of steel. Straddling him, she made it impossible to throw her over or even off him.

She smiled in his face and displayed a grin with no teeth on the top row. There were only two on her lower jaw, but the distance between them made it impossible to believe that either of them actually did her justice when it came to aiding her in consuming meals. She exposed an abnormally long tongue that she used to lick the side of his face.

"I'll bet you're going to taste good. I love dark meat." She said with a grin.

She leaned forward and began to stab at him with kisses. He swung his head from side to side, avoiding her with every thrust of her huge

31

head. Finally he brought one of his knees up fast and hard. He watched as her facial expression slowly went from one of squint eyed fun to wide eyed pain. Along with the change in her mood, her body was also positioned higher in relation to his body. He took advantage of this and she released her vice like grip screaming. He rolled her off of him and now with the positions switched; she began kicking and screaming like her life was on fire. She started to reach for him. He avoided her as best as he could. Her face began to take on strange new expressions of joy, eroticism and anger. He let go of her male genitals and stood back.

She got to her feet and said, drooling as she swayed back and forth in a sort of wrestler's stance. "We've been waiting on you. What took you so long? You've missed some great meals."

He stood as ready as she was. She rushed him, full force like a locomotive. He ran towards her and launched a well aimed foot. She stopped and caught it. With his leg in both of her hands; she proceeded to swing him first into furniture and then into the wall. She then extended her reach and grabbed hold of one of his arms and threw him through the dining room door. He crashed into the chairs underneath the dining room table. As he slowly got to his feet, he became eye level with the dining room table. Penny was stretched across the table, covered in blood. Once he was standing Pearl burst through the door like a bull. She charged him and this time he didn't move. At the last moment he stepped to one side and took her off at the throat. The force of the move stopped her from the neck up instantly, while the rest of her rose off the floor. Her large body went into a flip as she landed face down on the floor. He turned and started to look for a pulse on Penny. It was almost none existent. He called for backup on his cell phone.

He looked at Penny and said. "Don't worry. You're going to be fine, just hold on."

He started to look around the house. He drew his gun and went up stairs. Along the spiral stairwell there was dried blood and different color strands of human hair. Once he reached the top of the stairs, he kneeled to take a closer look at some deep gouges in the Hardwood floor. The entrance to the hallway was like a crypt. The sounds and smells of it were almost too much to bear. As he passed by a bedroom doorway, he notices a torso nailed to the wall. The condition of its appearance leads him to believe that it must had been there a while.

The covers started to shake. It rose up into the air and seemed to hover in one place over the center of the kings sized. A feeling fell over him, causing him to turn, dropped to one knee and draw his weapon. The covers moved left and then right. The covers suddenly stopped and then continued the same movement all over again. He reached out with one hand and took hold of the covers. He gently pulled the covers towards him. A dirty dishwater blond face was uncovered. Her hair was long and it covered most of her body. He gently removed the strands of hair and revealed a tormented smile underneath. Along with her tongue and one of her legs. It was clear by the child like smile frozen on her faces; she had been robed of her mind. Afraid she would fall, he laid her down on the bed. Kneeling over her on one knee, he still couldn't help but feel a deep sense of pain for her.

A hand reached out and took hold of his arm, pulling him down into the matrices. He struggled against it but he began to sink. He pushed her off the side of the bed as he went down deeper and deeper. He starts to disappear a portion at a time. First his knees to his waist, as arms reach up and take hold of more of him. He struggled against whoever it was. Finally, except for his arms that held his weapon, he all but disappears from site. Soon he is totally swallowed by the matrices.

The girl manages to make it back to a standing position. She watches as the matrices shakes, stirs and violently jerks. The same hand that pulled him down into the bed, tears through the matrices wielding a jagged edged Bowie. The hand disappears and the matrices shakes even more violently than before.

Suddenly the bed comes to a complete stop. All was quiet. All was calm. One, two, three and then finally a rapid repeat of a cannon is heard. A series of blood splatters appear as the rounds tear holes in the matrices. They also continue as they blow holes in the ceiling. She watches as this bring down several large portion of plaster. They smash into bits and pieces as they hit the floor. The rounds also nearly hit her as she sat still positioned in the chair the room above.

Slowly a stream of smoke escapes from the center of the bed and the stranger's hand appears in the large gap in the center of the matrices. Tired he pulls the rest of his body from the matrices. He looks over at the little blond girl, who still stood there with the same grin on her face, and was now staring at the ceiling. He continued to climb out of the bed the rest of the way. He couldn't see anything, but he continued to go and check it out anyway.

He found the entrance to the third floor behind hidden behind an enormous book shelf in the other bedroom at the end of the hall. He found the same human claw marks along the walls as he had seen in the first stairwell. This time some of the gouges still had human nails embedded in them. He got to the top of the stairs and found a locked metal door. The lighting was dim and he could barely see anything, but he was able to make out the key hole in the door. He went to work on the lock and as he was in the process of opening the door, it was snatched open. A figure rushed him knocking him down the stairs. As they were airborne from the top step of the stairwell, the two of them exchanged blows in mid air. Each one giving the other firm information on how they felt about one another. One moment the figure shoved the stranger into the wall. The force was so strong the stranger's body made an imprint in the wall upon impact. The stranger responds by giving the figure a blow to the throat, and knee to his groin area. This causes the figure to bend over trying to absorb the blow. The stranger takes the opportunity to jump up two steps and special deliver a kick to the figure's face.

Upstairs she hears all that has taken place up to this point. The door slams shut and the stranger sees this from the stairwell.

"What a fucking hero." A voice said to her ear.

He said; "Fucking cops are all alike. All over the world, they all think their fuck'en invincible."

He continued on to say. "None of them are really considered a challenge. Although, some have only been able to be anything other than an annoyance from time to time. So, even though this one seems to be lasting a little longer then usual. If I were you. I wouldn't get my hopes up."

The two wrestle back and forth aimlessly. The figure grabs the stranger in the throat and with enormous strength, lifts the stranger off his feet, slamming the back of the stranger's head against the wall. The stranger, able to feel the wall against his back, responds with slamming the figure into the wall with the aid of both of his feet. The figure is broken and the stranger lands back on his feet. Angry the stranger charges the figure again, slamming him into the wall. The stranger throws a flurry of punches to the figure's face and head. The stranger picks the figure up and throws him down the stairs.

The stranger feels around the steps for his weapon and finds it. He proceeds to the door at the top of the stairs. He jumps and kicks the door open. He enters slowly with his weapon leading the way. He finds a number of black curtains hanging from the ceiling in sections. The room had dim lighting and there was an odd smell that hung in the air. He searched as he walked the floor quietly. A gust of wind blew through the curtains and he could see a chair sitting in the center of the room. He approached her and instead of assisting her, he walked right past her chair looking for something. She watched him as he stood off to her right. Her body was trembling and the chair started to vibrate. He turned and looked at her. Her face was filled with sweat and pain. He walked around her chair and saw a cable. He grabbed it and tore it out, the chair went dead. He walked back around to the front of the chair again.

Standing with his gun in his hand, he looked into the black curtains and said. "I know that you're there."

The voice spoke back; "I guessed that after you didn't come looking for me."

The stranger said; "Why don't you just give up?"

The voice laughed and said; "Now you're a bright boy Detective. Don't pretending to be stupid now. It doesn't fit what you've shown the two of us this evening."

Downstairs the officers arrive and confront the figure as he stands up. The officers attempt to take control of him. He quickly breaks one of the officer's neck and throws two more through a window. With the search lights and gum ball lights from the various patrol cruisers parked outside the home, the room is quickly illuminated. The other officers start to take him on again and change their minds when he breaks the back of another Officer with a bear hug. He flings the officer's body across the room and the other officer's open fire on him. They stop and once he falls to the floor they start calling for more assistants!

The shots are heard along with the sound of the patrolmen storming the stairwell. The voice says. "Detective, I'm afraid that this will have to be sorted out on another day."

The curtains all rush towards him as he drops to one knee and opens fire. Empty he drops one clip and reloads as he springs to his feet and bolts through the hanging curtains. The smoke and the sound of thunder from his muzzle filled the room. The curtains are filled with flaming holes from the hail of rounds of his cannons. As he nears the other end of the room he can see a dark figure disappear into a huge round opening in the center of the wall. At high speed he drops another empty clip and recharges his weapon. He sped up to close the distance. He could see the opening start to quickly shrink in size. He continued sending rounds into the opening as it got smaller and smaller. He reaches the wall with only a small portion still closing. It seemed to close slowly at first, and then it started to go faster. Peering into it he could see a massive tunnel lined with torn human corpses.

Angry he stands in front of it... His canon at his side, locked in the open and empty position. The muzzle smoking as it cools. He hears the same voice as before speak to him from within the small opening. "Now that was impressive. I look forward to seeing you again Detective."

Soon the hole is closed completely and all that's left is a wall of flesh. Filled with various faces, arms, legs and other body parts that quivered and shook. The wall of flesh pulsated with the pain of its victims. They scream and cry out in torment to him for help. There wasn't anyone else present who could hear and feel their pain. This was a door. A doorway to hell and it was closed. At least for now. He examined the wall and he could see it was lined with bleeding flesh and he could also see that it was riddled with the bullet holes from his weapon. The blood seemed to flow up the wall like tears.

In a rush the officers charge up behind him. A couple slip on the blood soaked puddles on the floor and land at the stranger's feet. The other officers join him and demand that he drop his weapon. After a moment or two of strong concentrated staring, trying to figure out what happened; he slowly turns and provides positive identification. He walks back to her chair and starts to set your mother free. The officers didn't find any sign of another person in the room. That night he saw her to the hospital in the ambulance, along with the other women who were also rescued. After a guard was posted outside of her room, he sort of disappeared.

Uncle Aaron said; "Later, after everything was over and the media let the story die down, she started calling the station to thank him and that's when she discovered that he had been suspended pending a termination hearing."

Uncle Aaron said. "Can you believe that? I mean, this guy rescues your mother and some other women from a family of serial murderers and he's reprimanded and ordered to turn in his gun and shield awaiting to be fired."

"I just don't like the way they do things in the big city" Uncle Aaron said as he shook his head.

Danny asked; "What did she do? How did she find him?"

Uncle Aaron said; "Well, remember, your mother had all these connection. She made a couple of calls and she was given his home address in about fifteen minutes. She went there and the two of them hit it off every since. My mother was worried, but after she moved in with him, she worried less."

"Why did she leave?" Danny asked.

Uncle Aaron replied. "I don't know, but I wish I did. The two of them were happy with each other. When I visited them, back there in St. Louis, they didn't even argue and when your mother came home she wouldn't tell anyone anything. Now she was real upset for a long time, but she got better at dealing with it over time. That's when I promised to help her with you, when you got old enough. I couldn't believe that I was supposed to help you. At the time I remembered you were built like a little tank. I wanted to take you over to a couple of guy's houses who owed me money, just so you could beat the day lights out of them with your rattle. But like I said the only one who can help you with this is your, mom. Even though she seems to have gotten over her, my mom always says that your mom's not fooling anyone. She knows that she's still in love with him. Your grandmother always said that with real love, you can't escape."

Just then the two of them heard sirens and jumped to their feet and ran back into the house.

CHAPTER 6

"Is she in?" Nicole asked.

"No she's not, but when she gets in I'll be happy to tell her that your boss wants to see her." Marsha replied.

Nicole looks at Marsha and says. "Marsha, he already knows that she's here. So just have her come out of the office and I'll walk back with her."

Marsha, says in a stern voice. "Look, I don't particularly like being called a liar, at least to my face. So you can say what you want to when you get back to him, but I'm telling you that she's not in. Plus how would he know that she's in any way! The man never comes out of his office. Does he have the whole building wired for camera and sound? Because if he does, I'm sure the Police, the F.B.I. and God knows who else, would like to know."

Nicole just looks at her angrily, turns and storms out of the office. As she stomps down the hallway she hears the last words of Marsha echoing behind her. "Some of us would really like to know. I mean, since he knows everything like when someone's in or out."

Once the door closes and Marsha is no longer in sight. Marsha locks the door and knocks on her boss door as she walks in, she finds her boss sitting on the front edge of the desk, staring down at her shoes.

After a moment, Marsha says. "Well you heard."

"Yeah, I heard." Her Boss replies. She takes a moment longer to stare at her shoes.

Marsha says. "I can call her and just say that you called and said that you won't be in today. Your feeling very well."

"No thanks. I'd better deal with this before it gets any worse." She replies.

She stands and straightens herself up and starts towards the outer offices. As she walks she reflects on how she came to be her, in the first place. The road from here to St. Louis Missouri, was paved with good intentions and she never thought that she'd be back her again. Especially after all that it took just to leave here to begin with. It's strange how things work out. Sometimes just when you think that you have everything under control, something or someone always happens to screw it up. She reaches the outer offices of her boss and Nicole is seated at her desk on the phone with the pieces centered in her ear. She enters the office and waits for a moment.

"Nicole where is he?" She asked.

"He's in his office trying out his new Japanese putter that just got here this morning. He was in a nasty mood until it was special delivered by messenger." Nicole answered.

She asked. "Who sent it?"

"Tashi. What happened last night?" Nicole asked.

"Nothing," she said as she opened the door and walked right in.

She could see him sitting in a large chair at the far back part of the office. As she passes through the sections of the spacious lofty office, she looks around at a few different exhibits that caught her attention. It's been a while since the last time she was here and it's obvious that he's added a few pieces to his art collection, which wasn't unusual for him. He was always known for buying things. All kinds of things and people, It was all the same to him. After all, Carlton T. Sai is a third generation millionaire, who's been bred to rule the world or at least his own little portion of the world. She finally reaches his chair and at first he doesn't acknowledge her as he continues to examine the shiny new putter. She stands patiently awaiting his response, watching him as he occasionally stops to think from moment to moment. He lays the putter across his lap and leans over and takes a large glass of brandy from the end table.

He sits back swirling the brandy around the glass, taking a whiff of its strong hypnotic bouquet. Then he says. "Why hello there, please take a seat. It's nice that you could join us. I'm sorry that we interrupted your morning routine. Oh yeah that's right, your just getting in. Was it a hard night?"

Sitting, she crosses her legs and folds her arms in front of chest and say's. "What did Tashi tell you? Didn't he have a good time? Didn't things go as planned?"

Carlton takes a sip from the glass and slightly tips his head back as he slowly swallows and says. "Well actually, I haven't really spoken to him yet. But his colleagues sent me this nifty brand spank new putter. Although I don't think that I'm ready to give up on my own twelve different set of expensive putters. I'm willing to try this one out for size."

"I'm glad to hear that things worked out for you." She replied with a blank look on her face.

Carlton quickly responded. "Are you trying to imply that I had something to do with what ever happened between Tashi and yourself? Because I didn't, but also at the same time I do admire an employee's ability to take the opportunity to show me some initiative or at least their appreciation."

Laughing she responded just as fast. "Is that what your calling it now an days? Because the law still calls it by its old name and just what appreciation do you feel that I owe you?"

Carlton leans forward in his chair and with an angry voice says; "When I found you, you were unemployed. You had a family and now your game fully employed with a generous salary and spacious corner office, all complete with a secretary. Why, you even have your own covered parking space. And now you piss all over a deal that I've been working on for the last three weeks!"

With flames in her eyes she stands with arms stiff and her fist clinched tightly at her sides, says; "There seems to be some kind of mistake around here! If you think that you found me lying in the gutter, then you're wrong! Also, you seem to think that I had no options and that's a lie! Now if you thought that when you hired me, you had a desperate stupid little intern, you couldn't have been more wrong!"

Frustrated and angry she turns and starts walking back towards entrance way. He yells. "You busted his balls, literally!"

Without even losing a step or stopping to turn around and answer, she yells back. "Send him a bag of golf balls and some Salve!"

Now back at the office, she swings the door wide open and storms past Marsha's desk. She was moving so fast, the wind that followed her knocked some papers right off her desk. She slams her office door and Marsha sits wondering if she should go in or not. Marsha waits an entire three minutes and decides to knock softly and enters her Bosses' office. She finds her Boss sitting in her chair and staring out of the glass wall that the skyscraper is incased in. The view is spectacular; it shows off the neighboring skyscrapers with a breath taking ocean view. Marsha enters into the room as quietly as she can.

As she nears the desk, her eyes were fixed on the back of her Bosses chair located on the opposite side of the desk, her Boss speaks. "Marsha, is there something that I can help you with?"

"I just wanted to know if you were alright and do we both still have a job?" Marsha asked.

"You can relax." She answered.

Marsha said. "I also want to say that I'm sorry if I made something already bad, worse."

She said. "Yeah, well don't be. What happened today was going to happen even if you had called in sick."

"Well, what happened or do you mind me asking?" Marsha asked.

Her Boss sat motionless, not saying a word. After a few moments Marsha began to figure that her Boss was giving her an answer to her question. Marsha started to think to herself about her Boss Ms. Lillian Polezogopoulos. Around the water cooler the other girls had asked Marsha about her mysterious Boss before. What she was like to work for. Was she moody or evil as the other female Bosses. Most of the girls feel that the women Bosses always go out of their way to be three times as tough on secretaries, just to prove that they're not all sitting at their desks doing their nails and primping their makeup. But even though her Boss was nothing like their horror stories, she was still a mystery to even Marsha and she had been working for Ms. Polezogopoulos for the last year and a half.

"O.k. if we're not in trouble, then why are you sitting in this room like this?" Marsha asked.

Still her Boss doesn't utter a word.

Finally, Marsha says. "Lillian, why what's the matter? I hate when you get in these little moods when your deep in thought. You're either worried about your baby boy or your stuck staring at that picture of that good look'en man that you keep hidden and locked away in your top desk drawer. You know if you tried talking to someone instead of keeping things all locked up inside, maybe you'd feel better."

Her Boss replied. "Better than what and just what kind of thing am I keeping locked up?"

"That's fine. That's o.k. You want to work things out for yourself, in your own way. O.k. I was just trying to help." Marsha replies.

"Marsha if you want to help me then just do your job and that will make everything else go much easier." Her Boss stated.

Marsha, disappointed at her bosses response stated; "Yes maim." And proceeded to exit the office and return to her desk.

Lillian continued staring out of the window for a moment longer and when she turned around, she opened the top drawer of her desk and placed a photo inside it and once she closed it, she locked it with a key.

CHAPTER 7

"Hey thanks for the ride, Danny." Said Mr. Lesko.

"Oh, that's o.k. Mr. Lesko." Danny replied.

"Hey, Do you mind if we stop over at The Duck Sauce?" Mr. Lesko asked.

"Sure." Said Danny.

"I have to get something to eat for my Dad." Mr. Lesko explained.

As the two of them entered the establishment they saw that it was packed with people. The Duck Sauce was a little place but it was well known for its great food from the sirloin porter house steak cuts and sea food gumbo to its famous name, roast suckling duck complete with its great sauce. Folks came from as far away as Los Angeles, San Francisco, Las Vegas and even further away like New York and Chicago. It was the place that you had to go to for the best food in this part of the land.

The two decided to get a table, seeing as how a to go order would take quite some time to get. As they waited for a waitress, Mr. Lesko lit up a cigarette and began staring at the menu for something inexpensive.

Mr. Lesko, saw Danny searching and said. "Hey, Dan."

Danny looked up at him and Mr. Lesko said. "Hey, just order what you want. It's on me."

"You don't have to do that Mr. Lesko, I've got money." Said Danny.

"I know, but I appreciate the ride home and you already said that you didn't want any gas money." Mr. Lesko replied.

Danny started looking through the menu once again, determined to find something inexpensive, but that also looked good.

A voice above him said. "Excuse me sir, but are you ready to place your order? My name is Dene and I'll be your waitress for this evening."

Danny looked up and immediately recognized that it was the same girl who waited on him at Madelyn's, across the street. Danny started thinking to himself that she must be working in both places.

Mr. Lesko started to place his order and also the one for his Father. Danny couldn't help but stare. He started studying her face, the soft smooth curves of her cheeks and the way that her bangs hung down over her eyes. She slammed her pen and ticket pad down on the table and apologized as she struggled to untie and then retie her hair back up again. After she had successfully completed the task, she quickly took possession of her tools once again, ready to do battle. Finally the silence had begun to betray him once again. Danny couldn't help it. He wanted to talk, but when he tried to open his mouth, his lips wouldn't work. He tried to force them, but the hinges on both sides of his jaw had rusted shut and he thought he would need a blow torch and several cans of oil to break them free.

Mr. Lesko realizing that even though Danny was a quiet person, even for him this was too silent said; "Ah, he'll have the spaghetti and meat balls. Please".

Still attempting to get the rest of his order, she said. "Do you want any of our triple cheese garlic bread with that?"

Danny still couldn't bring himself to answer. So Mr. Lesko said; "Yes, he'll also have some of your delicious three cheese garlic bread."

Dene now confused and amused looked at Mr. Lesko and said; "Will he have a Coke or what?"

The two looked at Danny who with the same look on his face managed to slightly nod his head in agreement with the proposition of a Coke.

As she started writing the rest of the order down Mr. Lesko said; "Yeah, Dene. It looks like that Coke one will be his selection tonight. So if you would be so kind as to bring that over as fast as you can. I know that he'd appreciate that. O.k?"

"O.k." She replied.

Off she went to place all three orders and totally embarrassed, Danny covered his head in his folded arms table. He wanted to just die from the shame of it all.

"Well that was interesting." Mr. Lesko said.

Danny still didn't move.

"Hey, tell me. Is it all women in general or is it just that one in particular that makes you lose the gift of speech?" Mr. Lesko asked.

"Just that one." Danny answered.

"Look, the only thing that you have to remember when it comes to women is, they're just as nervous to meet you as you are to meet them." Mr. Lesko said with confidence.

Just then Dene walked out with a plate of food. She proceeded to a table filled with unruly drunk men. As she bent over to serve the large platter of oysters on the half shell, one reached across the table and grabbed her boob. Another slipped his hand under her dress and lightly felt the inside of her thigh. Reacting quickly, she grabbed a large pitcher of beer and threw it into the face of the one who grabbed her boob and then turned and broke the platter over the head of the other.

Then still standing calmly at the table, as though nothing had happened, she took out her ticket book and said. "Well now, gentlemen. That will be $29.99 for the oysters. Plus four large pitchers of beers comes to $34.80. Which brings the entire check to the grand total of $64.79, that of course doesn't include tax. Please see the cashier on your way out and thank you. Please drive safely."

After both of them witnessed the events at the table, just four feet across from theirs, Mr. Lesko leaned forward and said. "If I were you, even after say like fifty years or so of marriage, I would still ask her if it was alright to kiss her goodnight."

Danny sat with his mouth wide open and his jaw dragged the top of the table as he swung his head back and forth in disbelief. His eyes were as wide as two large silver dollars. She returned with their plates of food and saw that Danny's mouth was still hanging wide open. She placed the large dishes of pasta on the table and reached over and lifted Danny's jaw up off the table.

She cleared her bangs out of her face once again and said. "I'll be right back with your drinks."

"Do we have a choice?" Danny thought to himself.

As she turned to walk away, Mr. Lesko leaned forward once again and said. "Just, to be safe."

Later, after finishing their meal, Mr. Lesko paid the check and Danny took him home. Once they reached Mr. Lesko's home. Mr. Lesko invited Danny in for a while. They both entered the front door and while Mr. Lesko disappeared down the hall. Danny saw a display of weapons on the wall of the living room. He entered the large living room and saw an even more impressive display of weapons on another wall to his right. He didn't think that it was wise to go any further so he stopped at the sight of the first display. Standing in front of the display, he studied a seventeenth century Japanese sword. It's mixture of fiery colors and sleek design gave off a vibe of absolution and swift certainty. He doubted its wielder rarely met its match. The condition of the magnificent weapon demanded a role of its commander to have been both its master and its slave as well. Through all the books on the ancient arts and cultures, such a relationship of oneness between a pair like this would develop a superior will, discipline and intellect. A lot of them were nearly driven insane with life such as it is today. They are like carefully loaded deadly weapons with no war to exercise their skill. Their pressure was and still is too great to bare, both way back then and nowadays.

Danny stood mesmerized by its glow until a presence drew his attention and caused him to look behind him. Beside him a man stood nearly four feet tall. He was positioned on the coffee table standing with a very large Bowie in his right hand and his left hand poised ready to strike. Danny stood breathless at the sight and did not move a muscle. He thought that if he tried to explain why he was there, the short man might take it as an attempt to launch an attack against him. Not knowing what to do, Danny stood still. Suspended in animation, in space and time, he was trapped. What the short man did not possess in size, he more than made up for it in his appearance. His face contained a scar that ran from the right side of his cheek, up along the bridge of his nose, and it continued through the center of his forehead. A streak of silver hair began in the center of his head and ran to the middle of his scalp, marking the trail of the rest of the scars path. The expression on the short man's face was blank, void of any emotion. But his steel blue eyes were nonetheless trained on Danny. Neither one blinked, each out of the other need or necessity for their own state of being.

"Dad, what are you doing?! He's one of the kids who works with me at the restaurant!" Said Mr. Lesko, who was screaming at the top of his voice.

"Will you leave the kid alone?!" Mr. Lesko demanded.

With grace the short man took a less threatening posture and tucked the large bowie away behind him, bowed and in a thick accent said; "I'm sorry if I scared you young man, usually my son doesn't bring anyone home with him. But I suppose there is a first time for everything."

"Small wonder." Mr. Lesko remarked.

His father jumped down from the table and as he passed his son on his way to the hallway, he muttered under his breath. "I don't know why you're getting so bent out of shape, I didn't hurt the little guy."

Mr. Lesko said; "I'm sorry about that, Danny. Lately he's been sick and I thought that he was still too weak to be up and around to his usual shenanigans. But I guess I under estimated him as usual."

"His accent, where is he from?" Danny asked.

"It's Hungarian and he's only been living with me for the last fifteen years. I mean, you'd think that it would have faded off even a little. But no way. Not at all, he still sounds like he did the day when I pick him up from L.A. Ex airport."

"And I'll never lose my accent, even if I live to be a million years old." Said his father as he passed Mr. Lesko again in the hallway, but this time he was headed in the opposite direction.

Mr. Lesko sat down at the dining room table while his father started eating his dinner. It was clear that the two, in spite of their differences were actually very close.

"So, your name is Danny?" Asked Mr. Lesko's father.

Danny responded with a nod of his head.

"The reason I asked, is because generally it's more customary for people to be introduced. But my son seems to have forgotten his manners once again. Something that I find myself reminding him of time after time again." Said Mr. Lesko's father.

At first Mr. Lesko had just started to read the news paper, but when a familiar feeling of being chastised fell upon him he quickly put down the paper and said. "Dad this is Danny. Danny this is my Dad, Mr. Gustavo Lesko."

That being said, Mr. Lesko looked at his father as though he was mentally saying, o.k.?

His father responded with a equal expression as if he were mentally saying, better late than never.

"Danny, just call me Gustavo. It's alright. O.k.?" Said Gustavo.

Danny nodded his head once more and Gustavo said; "Well I don't think your still stunned, so unless you don't have a tongue, just say o.k."

Danny said; "I understand, sir and I'm sorry if I upset you in any way when I went into to living room to look at those weapons."

"That's alright Danny, it's just that I don't want anything to happen to you and I would have to explain to your parents that you got hurt because you were not being supervised. Said Gustavo.

"Your dad and mother would really be upset and as one father to another, I just don't want to give bad news to anyone else's parents again. I'm retired from all that." Said Gustavo.

"So, school's out for a while. Are you enjoying your summer?" Gustavo asked.

"Yes sir." Danny answered.

"No, please just call me Gustavo. I'll never be a sir as long as I live." Gustavo said while chomping on an ear of corn.

"So, how is your mother?" Gustavo asked.

"She's fine." Danny said with a strange look of curiosity on his face.

Gustavo understood the peculiar look that he received from Danny and said; "Ah, I'm a bit old fashioned. So even though I don't know your parents personally, I still ask about them."

"Well my mom is fine." Danny answered.

"And in this country most folks seem to quite easily forget about him. So, how's your Dad?" Gustavo asked.

Danny hesitated for a moment and both Gustavo and his son picked up on this. So Gustavo said. "If my question bothers you its o.k. to just say that you don't want to talk about him. Cause, like I said, most folks in this country are raised quite differently than I was."

Danny said with his head hanging low over his chest. "It's not that. I just don't know that much about him. My mom and I moved here from St. Louis and I hadn't seen him since I was very young. I don't even know what happened between them."

"Danny, this seems like it's difficult for you to talk about. So, you don't have to." Said Mr. Lesko.

"Sure, that's right." Gustavo said, agreeing with his son.

"I mean, the way that this country is, you may never know who he is and by the time you manage to find out; it's either too late or you find out that your mother did you a favor. Either way, usually in life, you will find out. Unfortunately, very few of us are able to find out some of the answers to life's questions early. Some of them good or bad have to be answered and if we're blessed we have the time and the strength to except them. And from that point go on with our lives." Gustavo explained.

Danny said; "All I know is that he's some kind of Federal Investigator back east. All my memories of him are good. He was fun and he always seemed to be there when I needed him. I remember laughing with him and my Mother a lot, but I can't seem to remember what was so funny. But then one night I woke up and everything was different and it's been that way every since."

Danny then stopped talking as he again meditated over the visions of the nightmares that one by one started to play back and forth in his head. He didn't dare tell them for fear that they would think that he was crazy or something. He thought to himself that Mr. Lesko would probably think that he was some kind of sicko and fire him on the spot. Also, even though he believed that Gustavo was truly every bit of the caring man and father that he seemed to be, he felt that he had to be on guard again.

Gustavo said; "Danny, from what it sounds like to me, your father is a rare breed of man and from what I know about those type of men is no matter what happens in life, you can depend on them to do the right thing till their dying breath. Also, if I had to guess by judging your age, since he hasn't straightened things out with you yet then something is holding him up, but he will straighten it out as soon as possible. Unless it's got something to do with you in some way of course, and even then it's not going to keep him any longer than he has to."

Later the two of them walked Danny out to his car and Gustavo asked. "When was the last time you saw your Mother?"

"This morning." Danny answered.

"Well then she must know that you're not still at work and she might be getting worried about you, so you should be getting home now. O.k.?" Said Gustavo.

"Yes sir. I mean Mr. Gustavo." Danny closed the car door and as he drove off thought to himself, my Mother doesn't worry about me when I'm awake. She only worries about me when I'm asleep.

Chapter 8

"Grandpa, can I have some ice cream?" Little Tommy said standing in the entrance way to the din.

"Grandpa, do you hear me!" Tommy still persisting as he walked toward the easy chair that contained the remains of the figure of a man.

He looks at his Grandfather who is slumped down in his chair. The man seems to be perfectly healthy by site, but still he is truly missing.

"Tommy, what are you doing?" She said as she walked towards him.

"Grandpa is asleep with his eyes open again, Grandma." Said Tommy.

She takes him by the shoulders and leads him out of the room saying. "Now Tommy, what has Grandma told you about your Grandpa.?"

"You said that sometimes Grandpa isn't feeling well."

"Uh hum." She replied.

Tommy continued. "And he may not answer me."

"That's right and what else did I say." She asked.

Tommy continued as she picked him and set him down on his favorite stool at the breakfast bar in the kitchen. "But it doesn't mean that he doesn't like me."

"And what else did I say?" She asked as she took a container of ice cream from the freezer and began spooning scoops into a nearby bowl.

"He loves me." Said Tommy as he started licking the ice cream from his spoon and the bowl of ice cream that now in front of him.

She sits at the table sipping on a cup of tea as the two of them talk further. Though the conversation is cheery, she can't help thinking about the past. How good things used to be. It's a different world from the one that her family once enjoyed. She doubts that those days will ever come back and each day of existence seems to be one of torment and shame.

She lost track of the time and noticed by the clock on the wall that it was now eight thirty. Tommy wanted to watch cartoons so she took him to the family room and turned on the large television. She knew that Tommy always liked the cartoon, especially when they were shown on the big screen. Now with him comfortable, she noticed him yawning as she left the room. She knew that it wouldn't be long before she would be tucking him in.

She lightly touched him on the shoulder. He sensed a pleasant familiarity and broke from his spell. He looked up into her smiling face.

She helped him out of his chair saying. "Alex, it's bed time."

"Oh, is it that late?" He said.

As they walked together he sees an I.B. League photo commemorating a particular place and time of his life and starts to weep.

She can feel his sorrow and says. "It's alright dear. It's alright."

She lies him down on their bed and begins to get him undressed. Trying not to take notice, she continues to dress him in his pajamas and pulls up over him. She looks down at him and wonders where the time has gone.

"I know that you're upset with me, Doris." He said.

"Don't be silly Alex. You haven't done anything wrong." Doris said hoping to leave the room.

"I did my best Doris. I just don't know what happened." He said weeping.

"Alex its O.K. You had to make a choice. If you hadn't decided to get involved when you did things would have gotten a lot more worse than just us.

"I'm sorry I let you down." He turned over onto his side, his back to her.

"Now you listen, Alexander Hernandez Venetis. You did what you had to do to save those children. Who knows this whole filthy business might still come to an end. The Lord has always had the last word. Now you've done nothing wrong. So, stop worrying about it all and get some sleep." She stands firm behind him.

"O.K. dear, you're right. I'll try and get some sleep." He laid in bed still upset, but silent.

She leaned forward and kissed him on the head and said. "Goodnight honey."

She checked in on little Tommy and found him asleep. She put him to bed as well and then proceeded to the sun porch. She speaks to God in a prayer and there alone with the sounds of the tide crashing against the shore; she started quietly sobbing with no one to see her or witness her pain. The waves and the night alone cover her silent torment.

CHAPTER 9

"I can't believe that you did that!" Lillian said as she screamed at the top of her voice.

"Hey, I told you I have to keep busy and trying to get this barbeque sauce recipe completed has allowed me that opportunity to do just that." Uncle Aaron replied.

"So, burning down your home was productive in your eyes!" Said Lillian.

"No, and I didn't burn down my house! So, stop saying that!" Replied Uncle Aaron.

The two notices Danny standing in the living room and they both say at the same time. "When did you get here?"

"I've been standing here for a while. Uncle Aaron, don't tell me that your house burned down." Danny said concerned.

"No, of course not and what the hell are you supposed to be?" Uncle Aaron asked as he gave Danny a strange look.

"A Chip monk." Replied Danny.

"I knew that." Said Uncle Aaron.

"How would you know what kind of animal he was? You, who tried to bathe and feed a pet rock." Lillian said as she walked into the kitchen.

"How much of the house burned down?" Asked Danny.

"It didn't burn down. Only a little of it burned." Said Uncle Aaron

As he began to explain further Lillian yelled from the kitchen. "A little, his entire living room is one big fat charcoal briquette!"

"Ah, come on! No its not! So, stop trying to say it is! Uncle Aaron replied screaming at the top of his voice.

He looked back at Danny and said. "My sister always blows things out of proportion."

"Uncle Aaron, are you alright?" Danny said with a face full of concern.

"Yeah kid, I'm fine. Except for your Mother making me feel like a world class idiot." Replied Uncle Aaron.

Suddenly there was a loud slam from the kitchen and the big sound of stomping footsteps that came afterwards caused Uncle Aaron and Danny to look at each other in complete terror.

As she entered the room she snatched some parts of a news paper off the dining room table. Danny and Uncle Aaron started to run but there was no place to go. The three circled the living room in frantic display of one big cat chasing two little mice.

In the middle of everything she stops and says to Danny. "And just why are you running? Mr. Polezogopoulos."

"I'm not running. I'm just trying to keep in shape for when track season starts again." Danny said laughingly.

"Oh, so you think I'm too old and you can out run me, is that it?" She said laughing as well.

Again laughing Danny said; "It doesn't matter if you're faster than me. I can still out ghost you on any day of the week."

Suddenly her face lost all expression and she stood straight up and said; "Where did you hear that expression?"

Danny saw the change in her and also straightened the position of his body and said. "Why, what's the matter?"

"Where did you hear that expression?" She demanded.

"Why, is there something wrong?" Danny said with his face filled with concern once again.

"Mom, what's the matter? Is there something wrong?" Danny asked as she slowly sat down on the couch.

He quickly ran around the furniture to get to her. Once he got to her, he sat down beside her and grabbed her arm and said; "Mom, what's the matter? What did I say?"

She placed her hands in front of her face and wiped away her tears saying; "I can't believe you fell for it."

And with that said, she began hitting him with the rolled up news paper. Laughing Danny tries to get away, but she pins him down on the floor and after she's finished she lets him up.

"Now, go take your shower and get ready for Dinner." She said as stood over him in a sort of superior posture.

Danny says as he begins to crawl towards the hallway; "I can't believe that I fell for that either."

Taking advantage of Danny walking on his hands and knees, she pretends to kick a field goal with Danny's rear-end as the foot ball. She stops just short of actually hitting him and instead she just pushes his butt with her foot.

"Ah man, Danny." Danny says as he gets to his feet and looks back at her as he proceeds down the hallway towards his room.

"I'm number one! I'm number one! I'm number one!" She chants until Danny disappears into his room.

As she walked back to the kitchen, her brother follows her. Once in they hear the shower running. She turns and looks at him and says. "Did you teach him that?"

"No, but I know where I've heard it before." Uncle Aaron replied.

"I didn't ask you that. What I asked you was did you teach him that expression?" Said Lillian.

"And I said no. But you better know that it's time that he find out about his father." Said Uncle Aaron.

"And how do you know that?" Lillian asked.

"Because, he's been asking me and I don't know anything." Replied Uncle Aaron.

"And why would he ask you?" Lillian asked.

"Because he doesn't want to upset you." Uncle Aaron replied.

"And why would this upset me?" Asked Lillian.

"Because." Replied Uncle Aaron.

"Because, what?" Asked Lillian.

"Because, no one knows why you came home. No one knows what happened between you and Sebastian. Hell, Mom and Dad still are lost about how to deal with the whole thing. Every time we all get together at our parents, Mom always goes around and makes sure that everyone remembers not to bring him up." Said Uncle Aaron.

"She does that?" Lillian said as she continued to stir the gravy.

"You know Lillian, everybody liked him when you brought him home. And that's not an easy thing to do. Hell, Dad even sat and talked with him about anything and everything, and how many times does he do that with me? Try never." Uncle Aaron said angrily.

Looking at him and responding sharply, she said; "Oh, don't give me that. You and Dad don't have a close relationship because he's still waiting on you to grow up. And that's why you and he don't have long talks about just anything and everything. So don't blame that on him."

Uncle Aaron also responded sharply; "Hey, what happened to you guys? Look at how you defend him against your own brother. I'm at least smart enough to know that whatever it is, it can't be all bad."

"And how do you know that?" Lillian replies.

"Because if he had mistreated you, Mom and Dad would have known it the instant you got off the plane. Instead you didn't say a word. You just landed and walked right off the plane and into the car like you've just been away at summer camp the last six years." Said Uncle Aaron as his voice got louder with every breath of anger he spoke.

Until finally she slammed the large spoon on the counter and said; "Look, you don't know what happened. None of you do and that's the way it's going to stay. I don't have to beg or get your permission to live my own life. And if me coming back here to live caused you and all of my family some problems then I'm sorry. Hey, I know, maybe I'll just move. How's that? Would that solve everything?"

"No, because if you did. I would miss your old cranky ass." Replied Uncle Aaron.

For a moment the two stared at each other and suddenly it was like they were twelve and seven years old again. The thought of all the memories and arguments over the years from bicycles and Barbie's to slumber parties and using the family car on Saturday night, made them burst into laughter.

Lillian said; "Not, to get off track, but also, just like you I don't know what happened between you and Tracy. For whatever reason, whatever happened, I still don't want you to create this great secret barbeque sauce in the comfort of your own living room any more. O.K?"

"Ah, man. Come on sis." Replies Uncle Aaron.

"Hey, all I'm saying is just not over an open flame any more. O.K.?" Asked Lillian.

"Oh, alright." Uncle Aaron agreed.

"And when you want to use an open flame, just go outside and cook. O.k.?" Lillian asked.

Uncle Aaron agreed as Danny returned from his shower. He was wearing a Soft Stone High School track team T-shirt that said, "Feet don't fail me now!," it featured a cartoon character running on a high school track and a pair of shorts. All was calm as they sat down to eat, but Danny could still sense it in the air. A feeling that heated words had been exchanged while he was in the shower, but since things seemed calmer now. He dare not break the peace, but he couldn't help but wonder.

CHAPTER 10

Beeeep! Beeeep! Beeeep! Tired of hearing it she finally hits the inter com button.

"Helen! Helen! Helen! Is that you?" A frantic voice screamed.

The voice continued on to say; "You had better be sick! Or else your ass is grass! I'm not going to cover for you at work anymore!"

Clorrissa said; "Hey, she's not here. So, stop yelling at my box!"

The voice was quiet for a moment. She waited for him to respond again, but there was nothing, not a sound. She decided to go back to what she was doing.

Until Beeeep! Beeeep! Beeeep!

"Hello." She says.

"Helen! Helen! Is that you?" The voice said.

Clorrissa recognized that it was the same voice and said; "Hey, I'm sorry but Helen isn't home."

She waited for a response but there was none. She said. "Hey, did you hear me? Is there a message or something that you want me to give her when she gets home?"

Clorrissa waited again for some kind of a response and again nothing came. She got curious and went to her TV to see if she could view who had been buzzing her box. As she grabbed the remote control and started to go to the channel that her building has reserved for closed circuit TV camera viewing, she thought to herself that it's another one of Helen's screw ball fans, leads, friends or coworkers from the news office. She got to the screen and all she saw was a view of the front entrance way's big wooden door. As she again started to get back to what she was doing, she couldn't help but think that as much money as she and her roommate pay for this apartment every month, they ought to be able to afford a doorman to screen unwanted guests.

She opened up her web site on her computer and proceeded to view her orders from the day. She couldn't get a rhythm going at first but she finally forgot about the male voice on her inter com system. She went on clearing large orders and setting up new ones as well. An hour or two passed by and her mind was fully emerged in her work. Nothing else existed in her universe. After all her internet work only paid the bills until she could complete her research on Dr. Theodore Hurston Grant. She was sure it would bring her the recognition that she had been struggling for and not to mention the funding for her future work.

Beeeep! Beeeep! Beeeep! Beee! Beeeep! Beeeep!

She ignored it thinking that this time they would get the message and just go away, after a while the beeping stopped. Feeling successful, she let out a sigh. A moment or two went by again and all was still stayed quiet.

Beeeep! Beeeep! Beeeep! Beeeep! Beeeep! Beeeep! Beeeep! Beeeep! Beee! Beeeep!

She couldn't stand it again. The aggravation was too much to bare. She swung around in her seat and stormed off towards the living room. She walked in and grabbed the remote off the living room coffee table and changed the TV station back to the closed circuit TV security camera channel. Although the beeping was still going on there was no one at the door. The view was only showing an empty entranceway with the same large wooden door. Now a little frightened she looked at the inter com system on the wall. She could view it plainly from where she was standing in the living room. She walked towards it and when she reached it, she hesitated on pushing the button. But then she thought that maybe the button was stuck or the system was malfunctioning.

She slowly reached for the button and pressed the button and said. "Hello. Is there any one there?"

There was no answer. Another moment or two past by and again she started trying to convince herself that it had to be one of Helen's screw ball aquatints.

She decided to ignore them again and just to let them know that she was serious she pressed the button and yelled; "Hey, whoever is playing on my inter com system, I'm warning you. You touch this button again and, I'm calling the police and they will hall your ass away. Whoever you are, this is your final warning."

She went back to work. Once the orders were completed, she closed the web site and proceeded to the computer files involving the incident at California college of University? After submitting her pass word to obtain excess, the protected file burst onto her computer screen.

"God, I hate that." She whispers underneath her breath.

The screen is full of bloody pictures from a class room that was hidden away from everyone at the University. Each scene was more gruesome then the last. Some of the walls were covered in human torsos and tissue. Notations from the Federal Forensic experts on the scene cataloged all types of herbs, spices, D.N.A. and all kinds of unidentified foreign substances and samples from months ago. She fast forwarded to another link and was stopped by another Federal Security Excess wall. She minimized the web site and excess her own e-mail and pulled a particular pieces of e-mail. It began with; "Someone must know the truth." A list of the Federal Forensic web sites were listed along with a map of which ones to avoid to guard against detection and suspicion.

Also, there was a list of pass words for each site. The e-mail was signed off in Latin, which when translated simply meant "May God Save The Innocent."

She figured out which one of the pass words went to that particular site and minimized the page. Returning to the Federal page again she applied the pass word and once excess was granted a whole new list of files burst out onto her screen. The files were listed oddly and it took her some time to read through most of them. After a while she went back to her own research paper to make notes.

Doctor Theodore Hurston Grant was a dedicated Professor of mythological cults. During his claim to significant notoriety, he has studied at some of the world's top I.B. league college Universities.

His discoveries have answered many of the unanswered questions for the Psychology & Criminal Forensic Justice Professions.

Theorizing that most cults view Psychopathic Behavior as a talent to behold as something of greatness, it is the ability to accomplish their tasks with the greatest of ease that is admired by them and not to mention their ability to detach themselves from their feats, no matter how demanding or tediously disgusting.

Dr. Grant's extensive studies have proven to be both enlightening and also horrifying. He uncovered the sources of so many of their beginnings that others, both colleagues & the Justice Department, theorize that it lead to his demise.

We may never know the events that lead to Dr. Grant's awful out come and why he chose to violate every decent notion to conduct his research within the perimeters of normal protocols. Perhaps the answers lie in sifting through the remains of his notes that were found between his home & office computers.

Currently it is taking teams of authorities and experts to try and retrace the steps that he took to get to this point. It should be noted that these are the very same experts that the good Dr. Grant once gave invaluable help to. The same experts that he assisted in every aspect of their profession.

At first, much like most predatory creature who exist, no one had a clue as to the secret experiments of Dr. Grant. Authorities were alerted to his actions by a tip that they received over the phone. Now considering the Professor's standing in the Analytical and Criminal world the phone call ordinarily would be thought of as a prank. The only reason that it was taken seriously was due to the identity of who was making the call. The call was made by the Dean of the University.

Dean Venetis would only say that the Professor had a group of small children and he was out of control. He went on to say that he didn't know where the Professor got them from but they needed to be rescued from him as soon as possible.

The first Detectives to arrive on the scene were Thomas O'Connell and Davy Lowe. The two met and spoke with Dean Venetis, who advised them that despite the Professor's distinguished history they should take every precaution when it comes to confronting him, he was dangerous. Dean Venetis knew that out of the two men O'Connell and the Professor were on first name basis. In the past the two of them had collaborated on a series of different personal matters. Only a few knew that they had this connection, but later during a interview and interrogation session he denied having any knowledge of their semi close current involvement. The Dean told detectives that he knew that the men were dead before they left his office.

It's been theorized that since the Detectives had shown up in the middle of the good Professor's class he felt that the serenity of his work had been violated.

Witnesses say that the two Detectives, armed with a map of instructions from Dean Venetis, walked straight through the campus grounds and entered Hopkins Hall.

Witnesses inside the hall say that the two Detectives were seen entering the closed section of the building. It was a section that had been under construction for almost three years. At first they knocked on the door and the Professor didn't answer. The Detectives were seen joking and laughing with each other as they continued to knock and wait for the Professor to answer the door.

Witnesses also stated that the Professor snatched the door open and laughingly invited the two Detectives in. Witnesses say that several moments passed by and then suddenly there were screams heard coming from the class room. Witnesses reported hearing the sound of the first voice screaming followed by rapid gun fires. The second sounds of screaming; didn't come til moments later. From what they thought to be the other Detective. When asked if there were any sounds of gun fire made after or during the second screaming voice; all witnesses reported no. Several witnesses all stated that the second sounds were different, like the other Detective was maybe waiting for his turn.

According to the witnesses and the signs at the crime scene, it's been theorized that due to Det. O'Connell's semi relationship with the Professor; the Professor decided to kill Det. Lowe first. Further theorizing assumes that in spite of the sounds of gun fire, the murder of Det. Lowe must not have taken very long, there by leaving Det. O'Connell in a mental state of shock. Also theorizing that the time that elapsed between the sound of both men screaming and not to mention the neatness of the class room, gives way to the thought or the idea that Det. O'Connell and the Professor either engaged in conversation or a slight stand off before the Professor murdered him.

Later the two men were found torn to bits. Their body parts were thrown out into the hall of the college like garbage. Dean Venetis was notified immediately and that's when he once again called for reinforcements.

Once Authorities were all in place the hostage negotiators went to work on attempting to talk the Professor out of the class room. Under further information obtained from Dean Venetis they also had reason to believe that the Professor had small children present in the class room.

Professor Grant refused to have any contact with the hostage negotiators. Both Federal Tactical and local S.W.A.T. Team Tech's, with the use of Hi Tech camera equipment, reported seeing the Professor walking back and forth in the class room bleeding profusely.

Both Teams also reported that the Professor was raving mad and kept repeating the same following statements; "It's my perfect creation. It's finally finished. It's my master piece, my life's work of art, on my very own canvass."

Both Teams also reported that as they continued to observe the Professor through fiber optic Hi Tech cameras they also discovered that he was missing his left foot, his right leg from the knee down and his left arm from the elbow.

At one point the teams started to storm the class room and take the Professor, but the Professor held them back with a stainless steel 50. MM caliber semi automatic hand gun. He had been wielding the large hand throughout the entire ordeal.

Special Agent Ren Elk, one of the Federal Negotiator's who was present outside the hallway of the class room, attempted to speak to the Professor. He asked the Professor about his master piece that he created.

Special Agent Elk said; "You know Doctor, no one will ever see this master piece that you're talking about."

"Why not?" The Professor replied.

"Because nuts like you always think that you've created something great when all you've done is just add to the world's problems." Answered, Special Agent Elk.

The Professor responded; "You know my boy. I've always had a soft spot for bright intelligent individuals such as yourself. You sound exactly like that fool who sits in his office thinking that he's safe in the world. Thinking that he and all the rest of the world have got things together. That God's in control of it all and all one has to do is call upon his name and he'll be there in an instant to save you. Well I have a surprise for God, you, that fool in his office and the rest of the world as well. My work is going to make itself known and all of you who snickered behind my back, like little school yard girls, will pay for it with everything you've got. Fortunately for you, bright boy, you won't be around to see it. No, I think I'll have you for myself."

Special Agent Elk responded by laughing and said; "Gee Doc, just how are you going to do that? I mean, do I have a minute to jerk off one more time or not?"

"I think not." Replied the Professor.

Later it has been argued by the Superiors of both Agencies that they didn't know which was stranger. The fact that Special Agent Elk decided to exhibit the mental strains stemming from the effects of a failed marriage or the fact that without any equipment or way of pin pointing his location in the hallway, the Professor was able to put a 50 MM caliber round sized bullet hole through the wall of the class room which also proceeded through the head of Special Agent Elk as well. Following that, the order was given and both Tactical Teams stormed the doors and took the class room.

Once the class room had been taken, Authorities discovered a group of children hidden in the rear of the class room. After the standard investigation and examinations the children's parents notified and they were reunited.

Analysts discovered evidence at both the Professor's office and home that suggests that he had done extensive research into the Mythological Dark Arts of several different continents. Including some areas in Africa, the Middle East, Haiti and the Caribbean.

There were large amounts of imported salt and other strange

imported substances that are still being analyzed. Not to mention the fact that both the office and the home contained a strange smell and were saturated with some kind of substance.

Analysts also uncovered, through materials obtained at both locations, information relating to the progressive scale of the Professor's ability to experiment on the children's mind, body and their very souls. According to the same information he had reached success when two of the small children had finally obtained the highest level of concentration of mind body and soul; the information also suggested that even though they both had obtained this heighten level of awareness. Only one was rebellious and uncontrollable. The Professor tried repeatedly to break the child's will, but the child would not submit to him. The last notes ended when the Professor discovered evidence that suggests that subject #1789 may have not only been already aware of this ability, but he may have also been able to control it as well.

As Clorrissa continued to type away at her computer the toes of her bare feet began to freeze. She stopped typing and looked down at the floor and saw that the floor was filled with water. She pushed her chair back and stood up. The office floor was full of water.

She slipped her feet into her sandals and started walking towards the hallway to look into the bath room. She thought to herself that it had to be coming from the sink or the tub.

Clorrissa splashes out of the room and as she makes her way down the hallway she notices that the floor of the hallway leading to the bath room was completely dry. She stopped immediately and looked behind her at the water. She could see the small ripples of water gliding towards her. A feeling of fear sweeps over her and she backs down the hallway towards the living room. The water is lighting fast as it splits into two rivers of waves and speeds past her and reforms itself at the entrance to the living room. She starts to look at it again as she backs away in disbelief. The water runs up the walls and starts to gather over her head. She turns to run down the hallway and slips and falls as the door to the office is slammed shut. The water takes hold of her and throws her down the hallway. The lights start to dwindle and she gets to her knees, crying and screaming she crawls into the hallway. She gets to her feet and jumps towards the front door. Franticly she tries to unlock the front door of the apartment. She can see the water racing towards her. She swings the door open and feels the icy water climb up the back of her legs and slowly makes its way up the small of her back. The water covers her face and a in the dim lighting of the hallway a figure is seen standing as she is snatched back inside the apartment. From the hallway her muffled sounds are heard. In the entrance way of the building, the inter com system begins broad casting her screams.

CHAPTER 11

It's a late weekend afternoon and Dene is preparing Madelyn's Gas and Food Mart for her shift. She's completed wiping down all the counters and making sure that the concession section has enough nachos, hotdogs and etc. Now she puts on a coat and goes into the freezer to stock the beer on the shelves.

Darla snatched the freezer door open and shouted. "When are you going to be done?"

Dene responded; "I'm almost done now."

"I have something else to do so hurry up." Said Darla.

Dene stopped and gave her a look that sent Darla back to the cash register. Dene started to rotate the stock so that she could finish stocking the cooler. The light started to flicker, which made her nervous. She thought to herself, Madelyn never cares about us employees; she wouldn't bat an eye if one of us fell down some stairs or got bit by a rat just because of the shitty lighting. As she continues to stock the shelves, cold air blows up both of her pants legs. She jumps up and turns around, only to be face to face with a large amount of fog in the figure of a face with a smile. A hand grabs her on the shoulder and she lets out a scream as she takes off running. She springs out of the entrance to the freezer and past all the food and customers.

Darla sees her in full sprints and yells; "Hey where are you going?!"

Dene bouts through the exit and sprints past the cars in the parking lot, she makes it across a crowd street and out on to the beach. Running at the speed of light, with the wind in her hair, she sails up the beach. Even maintaining her top speed she can still feel something behind her. Something prowling at the edge of her heels. As her feet hit the ground she could feel it's weight impact the sand behind her with every step that she made. As she neared Bobby's cliff, her thoughts were of freedom and of peace, sweet sweet, peace. She blew past the broken gate and with the edge of the cliff in sight she formed her body like a bullet and increased her speed. Suddenly her shoulders began to feel heavy. She started experiencing trouble maintaining her speed and balance. She tried to kick harder and harder to reach the edge until her body was so heavy that gravity pulled her to the ground. Her face buried in the sand, her eyes shut tight, all she could do was gasp for air. She started to choke and cough. A feeling of relief fell upon the tightened muscles of her shoulders. The same soothing feeling began to make its way down the center of her back and back up again.

A soft voice said; "I'm sorry that I scared you. I didn't mean to when I touched your shoulder back at the cooler."

She turned to see who it was and discovered Danny with his hand on her back. Afraid that he may incur the same wrath as those that he witnessed back at the Duck sauce, he quickly removed his hand.

She continued to lie still, so he also laid down beside her. She began to feel embarrassed about the whole thing and somehow Danny picked up on it.

Lying on his back and staring up at the clouds he said; "You know you don't owe any one anything. You don't have to feel bad about nothing."

He could feel her tension easing up and said; "And if you ever want to talk to someone I'd be happy to listen to anything that you've got to say.

He could hear her breathing start to even itself out and said; "And you know what? We don't have to talk at all. We can just lie here and do this all the time."

After a while she got up and the two started to walk back to Madelyn's. As they walked neither one said a word. Once they reached the store two Policemen stepped out of the door from Madelyn's and grabbed Danny. They slammed him up against the hood of the Police Cruiser. Officer Greager twisted Danny's right arm up into his back and held it there. At the same time that Officer Below preceeded to press the cheek of Danny's face against the burning hot hood of the Cruiser.

"But, I didn't do anything." Danny said, while trying to deal with the pain and not to mention the embarrassment.

"Hey, what the hell do you think that you're doing?" Screamed Dene.

"Well when we get calls that some moron is chasing a pretty little girl down the beach and she doesn't have a smile on her face; we usually like to make sure that it doesn't happen again." Responded Greager.

"Well there's no reason for you to treat him like that so just let him go." Said Dene.

Ignoring her and pressing Danny's face against the hood of the cruiser harder, Below replied; "Well are you sure?"

"Yes I'm sure." Dene answered.

Still pressing Danny's now red face against the searing hot hood of the cruiser replies; "Well just as long as you're sure."

Dene walks over to Below, looks him in the eyes and says; "If you don't take your hand off my friend's head, I will press charges against you for Police brutality myself."

Below could see the seriousness of her face and said; "The next time the two of you have a lover's spat don't call us again."

As the two of them let go of Danny and started to get back into their cruiser she replied; "And if I ever called for the Police it wouldn't be you two, because everyone knows that you're worse than criminals."

Below angered by her words responded; "Little girl you'd better hope that I never show up for another domestic call involving the two of you, because if I do, I'll take both your asses to jail and you can bank on that. Missy!"

As he sat back in the vehicle he turned and looked at Danny and said; "I'll see your ass again too, boy."

Danny looked at the cruiser as it slowly disappeared from site. As he started to walk towards his car, he glanced at Dene. The look on her face was blank and as he drove away, he couldn't bear to look back.

CHAPTER 12

"The meeting will now come to order. Will the secretary please read the minutes of the last meeting's?" Says the Chairmen as he takes his seat.

The minutes are read and the process of handling the issues of running a University begins. Later after the meeting is over, he leaves the conference room just as quickly as he entered.

His steps echo through the hallway alerting the attention of Barbara Oerb. Ms. Oerb catches a glimpse of him as he crosses a hallway, she chases after him. She turns down one hallway after another. She catches another glimpse of him as he corners another hallway. She's closer to him this time so when she turns the same corner she will finally catch up to him.

"I swear that this place is like a maze." She says as she turns the corner.

She finds herself standing in a dead end hallway. She sees a door and walks to it. She figures he went in here to avoid her. She snatches it open and four people rush her, knocking her down. She sits up and finds four large janitorial mops lying on top of her.

Sitting in his office, he waits for her. Ms. Oerb burst's through his office door. His secretary, closely in hot pursuit, takes Ms. Oerb's arm and commands her to leave.

"Why is it so hard to see you Dr. Kimbrel?" Said, Ms. Oerb as she was being dragged from the office by his secretary.

From the back of his chair he waived off the secretary with his left hand. The angry woman leaves the office. Standing in the center of the office floor Ms. Oerb is both shocked and slightly nervous. She never thought she would ever be successful in getting a meeting with the Dean of students Dr. Arthur T. Kimbrel. He has always avoided every kind of opportunity to be interviewed by the media. He even refused to be photographed by the University's society, stating that being photographed was against his religion. So the University has been looking into having his portrait painted. Tradition dictates that his portrait is to be displayed in the great hall among the previous Distinguished Deans. A place was reserved right next to his predecessor Dr. Alexandra H. Venetis.

"Well, Ms. Oerb. Just what can I do for you?" The chair doesn't move at all.

"Well for starters you can stop having people chase you through the halls, when all they want to do is talk to you." Said Ms. Oerb.

"I'm sorry I don't understand." Said Dr. Kimbrel.

Ms. Oerb's face lit up with aggravation as she responded with; "You mean to tell me that you didn't know that I was trying to catch up with you in the hall way just know? Or that for the last three months I've been trying to get an appointment to see you?"

"Well I apologize if my schedule is often tight, but after all I am the Dean of one of the most historic and prestigious Universities in California." Answered Dr. Kimbrel.

"But sir, a Dean should have time for his students. I understand that you have a busy schedule. But if it wasn't for us, the University wouldn't even be here." Ms. Oerb sternly replied.

"Well, you certainly have a point there. But it's getting late and I due have a busy schedule so as I said before. What can I do for you Ms. Oerb?" Said Dr. Kimbrel.

She started to answer but the strangest thing happened. She was totally clueless as to what she wanted to say. She struggled to remember but it was impossible. Her mind was a total blank.

"Ms. Oerb. Ms. Oerb. Are you O.K.?" Dr. Kimbrel asked again and again.

Ms. Oerb was mentally stuck. She kept trying to say something but it wouldn't come out. It slipped into a black hole and disappeared.

A hand reached for her and touched her on the shoulder. It startled her and she let out a scream that nearly sprang out of her skin. All of the air left her body and she started to lose consciousness.

She looked to see who touched her, but there was nothing there. The room started to go sideways as though she were on the deck of a ship in the middle of a great storm. Back and forth the motion went. Over and over the room rocked. Her body slowly became limp. She started to fight it, but it was too strong. Suddenly the ship couldn't handle the waves any longer and started to sink. An enormous wave took the ship down nose first.

The sea was black to her. She couldn't make out a thing as she held on to the side of the diving vessel. She started to shake her head as she tried to focus. She could make out something on the ocean floor. It must be a deep cavern she thought. But if it was then why was it in the shape of a gruesome grin. It's got to be her imagination. It's got to be. As the ship continued to free fall, she could make out two smaller openings above the hideous smile. And now she could see it. It's full face. The left eye winked at her and opened its smile wider. She panicked and jumped off the deck in an effort to make a swim for it. She heard a crashing sound beneath her and looked down just in time to see the ship being chomped to bits by the smile.

She looked up towards the surface and she could see that it was daylight. But how? Where was the storm? The distance was closing in as her body grew tired. She couldn't swim any more. Her arms and legs throbbed with pain as she slowly gave up the struggle to survive. By then the smile had finished consuming her ship and was now patiently waiting for her. It seemed to pull the water towards it, creating a current. Just as she started to enter its mouth, she started to struggle again. The face changed from one of delight to one of anger. It opened wider and wider as it increased the flow of water.

"Barbara, wake up! Wake up now Barbara! Do you hear me?! Wake up Barbara!" Barbara woke up only to find Paramedics yelling at her.

She was lying on the floor of Dr. Kimbrel's office. They picked her up and placed her on the gurney and started to wheel her out of the office. The motion of the gurney was like the ocean so she fought to keep her eyes open and grabbed the arm of one of the Paramedics as they continued. She looked at Dr. Kimbrel's secretary as they passed her desk. She seemed to have sort of a hidden smile on her face.

As they entered the main hall, the secretary stopped them and said. "Barbara here is your appointment reminder card. If it's not enough time and you don't feel well enough, then just call us back and we'll reschedule you for another meeting with the Dean."

The secretary watched as they wheeled her away and just before they turned the corner Barbara crumbled the note and threw it on the floor.

CHAPTER 13

Danny stood watching a family. The father was feeding the infant in the high chair. It seemed like no matter what the father did the baby continued to chew a couple of times and then spit the food all over himself. It was a mess and the mother said so when she returned from the rest room with the couple's five year old daughter.

"What's the matter?" Said Mr. Lesko.

Danny didn't say a word. He just continued to stare into space.

"Hey, what's the matter? Mr. Lesko said, but this time louder.

Danny snapped out of it and answered; "Nothing."

"Have you thought any more about talking to your mom yet?" Asked Mr. Lesko.

"No." Replied Danny.

"Well, you will when the time is right." Said Mr. Lesko.

The too stared a little longer at the family and then Danny brought them a couple of wet towels. Mr. Lesko started working on the ice cream machine. Danny stayed over to help him.

"So, what's going on with that little girl over at The Duck Sauce?" Asked Mr. Lesko.

Danny, lying on his back under the machine, pretended not to hear him and said nothing. Instead he asked; "How's your Dad?"

Mr. Lesko began to talk about how his father was driving him crazy. He said; "It's like living with, The World's Most Tiniest International Blood thirsty Commando. I mean I'm serious. I could be married to a hot little babe like that guy has. She could have been my wife and those could have been my kids, but noooo. I've got a little Hungarian razor back hedge hog, who enjoys wearing the ugliest pair of Bermuda shorts that I've ever seen, living with me. The hair on his back, when he walks through the house, looks like a giant Q-tip. He's not just the president he's also a member."

He stopped talking for a moment and when Danny didn't hear from him he started to feel a little odd. He continued to screw in a bolt to a door that houses the coolant system.

"Hey can I have the smaller screw driver?" Danny asked.

Slowly the screw driver made its way down to him. Danny held out his hand and when the screw driver met his hand he took hold of it. As he pulled on the screw driver he realized that Mr. Lesko did not let go of it.

"Hey, Mr. Lesko are you going to let go of the screw driver or what?" Danny said.

Mr. Lesko didn't answer and he still wouldn't let go of the screw driver. Finally Danny slid himself out from under the machine and sat up. He found himself face to face with a pair of bare, slender, shapely legs. Dene, who was holding the other end of the screw driver, was dressed in a body dress that showed off every inch of her young teenage figure.

She smiled and said. "Hi."

Danny stumped couldn't say a word. He laid his back against the ice cream machine and thought that he would play it cool and just give her the silent treatment. Actual he was really afraid. Afraid that he would open his mouth and make an even bigger mess of things than he had already. He settled for staring at his dirty arms as they lay resting on top of his knees.

The unspoken emotion between the two of them was so thick, you couldn't have cut it with a plasma blow torch. They were in love and it was so obvious a blind man could have seen it. Just the uncomfortableness, the sudden rise in body temperature and loud sounds of thunder that they're hearts made gave it all away. She stopped down beside him and lost her balance. She caught herself by grabbing hold of Danny's arm as he at the same time reached for her.

He got to his feet and helped her up. Her eyes again met his and neither one could move. For Mr. Lesko, watching the two of them seemed like an invasion of their privacy. They were in sink with each other.

She said. "I'm sorry about the other day."

"I'm the one who's sorry. I shouldn't have scared you in the first place." Replied Danny.

"Hey, I'm the one who freaked out and ran about a mile to jump off a cliff." Said Dene.

"Well if you had done it, I would have jumped in behind you." Said Danny.

"No, No, cause then there would have been too fools dead." Dene said.

Reflecting back on a night mare or two, while staring down at his feet, Danny said; "I can think of worse ways to die."

She caught the look on his face and said; "Wow, what's that all about?"

Danny shook his head and said; "Nothing."

"And I thought I had issues." Said Dene.

For a moment Danny's face started to look like he was extremely worried so Dene quickly said; "Hey, don't look like that. I was just kidding. O.K.?"

Danny's face started to lighten up, but he still seemed concerned. He said. "So, are you alright?"

Dene just smiled and said; "Oh, I'm fine. I just get like that some times."

"Like what?" Said Danny.

Dene smiled and said; "I don't know. I guess I just feel like letting go. That and I don't seem to like small spaces very much."

"So I take it that the freezer is small?" Danny asked.

"Very small. No Try extremely small. In fact let's just say tiny." Replied Dene as she chuckled.

Together with an understanding expiration, Danny also responded by nodding his head. They walked into the office where Mr. Lesko had left a message on the door saying;

Danny,

Please lock up and bring the keys back with you tomorrow.

Signed

Mr. Lesko

Dene, said; "Wow, either your Boss really really likes you or he really really trusts you.

"He and his Dad are really great people." Said Danny.

"Well, Madelyn would never give any of us the keys to the store and tell us just bring them back whenever we felt like it." Said Dene.

After the restaurant was locked up the two of them went down to the beach to take a walk in the moon light. As they walked along the shore beneath the stars, Danny couldn't believe his luck. At last he was with her and he felt like all his problems were finally behind him. For whatever reasons, the gods have smiled on him and he was never going back. As they walked, they laughed and stared into each other's eyes. Holding hands, they paused for moment and as the waves crashed against their legs they shared their first kiss.

CHAPTER 14

Danny walks into Madelyn's Food and Gas Mart. He sees Dene sitting in the center of the isle. She was rocking back and forth with her arms gripping her knees. He bent down beside her and saw that she was drenched from head to toe. The floor around her was completely bone dry and he couldn't figure out what she was saying.

"It's me. Dene, It's me. Hey what's the matter?" Said Danny.

He hesitated to touch her because of what happened the last time. She began crying and rocking faster and faster. Finally, he wrapped his hands around her and just hugged her as tight as he could.

"Please be alright. Dene, please be alright." Said Danny.

Her body had stopped rocking and he loosened his arms and moved back to look at her. Dene, looked him in the face and said; "You shouldn't be here. You'll get hurt too."

Suddenly the lights went off and Danny woke to find himself in bed. He jumped to his feet and grabbed his keys as he made his way down the hallway and through the living room. He left the front door wide open and as the wheels of his vehicle screamed out of the drive way. As he pulled away he saw his mother standing in the drive way watching him drive away.

Danny reached Madelyn's and slammed on the breaks. He saw that the lights were on as he got out of his car. There weren't any cars on the lot.

As she neared the entrance, he kept saying out loud. "Please God, no. Please God no."

He opened the door and slowly went inside. Danny walked in

looking for her. He didn't see her at the cash register, which is where she would usually be. He started searching for her throughout the isles of the store. Danny looked in the freezer and couldn't see a thing. He couldn't find her anywhere. He heard a loud thump and turned. It came from the rest rooms. He walked towards the door of the women's rest room.

"Dene, are you in there?" Asked Danny.

There was no answer. Danny started to worry more. He started thinking that if she was in there, suffering with an upset stomach, then everything was o.k. He opened the door there was no one there. Suddenly there was an even louder thump from the men's rest room. Danny stood still in between the men and women restroom doors.

Danny swallowed and said; "Please Lord make it O.K. Please God make her O.K."

He grabbed hold of the handle and took a deep breath. Danny turned the handle and as the door swung open he fell to his knees as he saw the entire men's room covered in blood. This was no dream. This was no nightmare. This was really happening and it was happening now, while he was awake, while his eyes were wide open. He was frozen at the site.

Just then he felt something cold on the back of his neck. He turned to look and heard as he was slammed to the floor. "Get down now! Get down now! Police Officers get your ass down now!"

Once Danny was down and his hands and feet were cuffed the Officers carried him out of the store. As his body swung back and forth his eyes filled with tears as he watched the remaining Officers begin to examine the men's room.

The Police cruiser reached the Soft Stone Police Municipal Station with Danny. Several Officers were waiting to grab and drag him out of the cruiser. They enjoyed occasionally stopping to slam him against a steel door or solid wall. Whether or not they knew it, Danny didn't care about the high level of abuse that they subjected him to. He just didn't care at all.

Finally he was placed in an interview and interrogation room. His hands were chained to the opposite sides of the steel table. The chain of the ankle cuffs was anchored and padlocked to the floor.

Danny lay weeping with his face on top of the cold steel table. A short time ago his life had begun and now a brief six hours later, it was all over. It came and left like a candle in the wind and he was now forever in tormenting hell. His mind started to shut down. Danny's spirit sank to the bottom of the room like a massive lead weight. He cried harder and harder. Screaming at the top of his silent voice, turning the enormous pain inward, it exploded over and over.

The door opened and Lt. Det. Jackson entered the room. He was a thin pencil of a man with a gray braided pony tail. His black shiny leather skinned boots and thin gray mustache were legendary in the Department. They knew him as the gray ghost. In his day he solved scores of cases. Jackson was the last of the old timers. The younger Detectives laugh and whisper behind his voice. But that doesn't worry him. Jackson knows what has to be done. Usually he can tell if a suspect was guilty or not within the first ten minutes. He took a seat at the opposite side of the steel table from Danny. He took out a miniature tape recorder and from his pocket he retrieved a Miranda rights card. He began reading and as he slowly called out each and every line. He watched as Danny didn't move a muscle.

"I know that it hurts, but I promise you that it will feel much better if you just talk about it." Said Jackson.

Danny didn't reply at all. His lifeless body continued to lay poured all over the end of the table. His tears ran into a puddle in the center of the table and dripped through a hole. As the tears fell they made loud splashing sounds as they hit the concrete floor below.

"Well, Lillian. How's it going?" Said Assistant Chief William Raft.

Lillian sat in a chair in his office refusing to exchange little repartees. With her arms and legs crossed she stared at him like he wasn't there at all. Her thoughts were with Danny. She needed to see him, touch him, feel him and make sure that he was O.K.

"Well, you're as quiet as your son. Neither one of you has anything to say about anything." Said Raft.

Lillian still maintained her silence.

"Well, that's O.K. too." Said Raft.

"I want to see my son." Said Lillian.

"Hey, well you can talk." Raft replied as he leaned back into his chair.

"Are you refusing me my right to see my son?" Asked Lillian.

"I'd almost given up hope on hearing that pretty little voice of yours." Said Raft.

He got up and walked around to the front of his desk and sat down. Admiring her figure he smiled and said; "You know, I hear that you went away to college and now you're back among all us small town people."

"Well, I'll just take that for a no." Said Lillian.

As she got to her feet, he stood up as well saying; "Hell, back in high school, I always knew that you thought you were too good for good old southern boys."

As she started to leave, she stopped for a moment in the door way and looked him in the face and thought to herself. These weren't Cops. Not real ones. In all of her experiences she had been in the company of all kinds and they weren't it. In all her life she had only really known one real one and now she needed him again.

CHAPTER 15

"Well, let's have it." Said Raft, as he entered the room.

Forensic tech Todd Sanders said; "I've never seen anything like it. The entire rest room was filled with blood. It covered the area of the ceiling four inches thick and it's still dripping as we speak.

"What are you telling me, you don't know how he did it?" Said Raft.

"No, I don't know how he did it. I'm stomped." Said Sanders.

As he started showing photos of the crime scene itself, he began his explanation of his examination of the rest room. Sanders advised that the ceiling was eight feet high and from corner to corner, the room was six by five feet in diameter. He also advised that there are no foot or finger prints.

Stewing in his seat at the other end of the table was Lt. Det. Jackson. Raft saw this and said; "Jackson, do you have anything interesting to add?"

Jackson seemed to shrink down in his seat as he hesitated to answer. He knew that Raft didn't think so much him. In fact he has been trying to get him to retire and give up his office, so he could put someone else that he has in mind for his spot on the force.

"Lt. Det. Jackson, do you have anything to add to this investigation?!" Yelled, Raft.

After a moment or two, Jackson frowned and sat up. He started to open the file in front of him; but instead he closed it and said; "Daniel Thomas Polezogoulos is a sixteen year old boy, who seems to be suffering from the trauma of either discovering the crime or..."

"Or maybe he did it!" Raft says sharply.

"Or maybe he did it, but I don't think he did." Replies Jackson.

"Oh, and why's that? Did he confess?" Raft asked.

"No, he didn't. Answered Jackson.

"So, you're telling me that he's claiming that he just happened to be there when we got there?" Replied Raft.

"Well, actually he hasn't said anything." Said Jackson.

"You mean to tell me that after all the time spent in that room with that fucking kid, you still haven't gotten him to talk yet?" Screamed Raft.

Jackson knew where this was going. He stood up and started sliding his chair into the table.

"Where the hell do you think you're going?!" Screamed Raft.

"I don't think he did it!" Said Jackson.

"Why's that? Did he tell you that? No he didn't! Why, because you can't get him to talk!" Argued Raft.

Jackson stopped and started yelling back at Raft. "Well, sir! If he did do it! Why is it he doesn't have one drop of blood on him! Not to mention that it is physically impossible that this boy could've done this! But, let's just focus on the fact that he doesn't have any blood on him at all! You can't do something like this and not be covered in blood as well!"

"So, what was he doing there?" Raft calmly asked.

"I'm not sure yet. I think that either the sight at the rest room was too much for him to witness or he must have known the girl. Then again, it could be both." Jackson answered sternly.

Back in the interview and interrogation room, Danny was still chained to the steel table top. He still didn't move as he heard the door open and slam shut.

"Well, you piece of shit wake up and get up!" Said a familiar voice.

"Come on wakie wakie. It's time to stop faking." Said another familiar voice.

"What's the matter boy? Oh, you're still all chained up. Here, let me help you." Said one voice.

The chains around Danny's hands and feet started to loosen. He still didn't care enough to open his eyes.

"Hey, I'm talking to you. So, sit the fuck up!" Yelled, one of the voices.

"Maybe he only likes fucking with defenseless girls." Said the other voice.

The two men grabbed Danny around the neck and arms and throw him over his chair. They slammed him up against the wall and he let out a scream to deal with the pain. He looked to see who the men were and discovered that it was the two Officers who gave him a hard time in front of Dene at Madelyn's. They enjoyed hurting him then, just like they're enjoying hurting him now.

"Well, I'm glad to see you awake." Said Officer Below.

Officer Greager punched Danny in the stomach and he bent over from the pain. Below, slammed Danny's head back into the concrete wall.

"You feel like talking now." Said Below.

The pain in Danny's head and stomach were tremendous, but it was nothing compared to the damage to his heart. Psychologically, he was lost with no way home. Not even his Mother could find him this time.

"Hello, hello! You're still not listening! I guess you need a little more motivation!" Said Below.

The two began working Danny over. They were careful not to leave any bruises as they pounded on Danny left and right. The two of them had perfected a skill of how to effectively inflict the maximum amount of pain and just how to get away with it.

After several blows to the back of Danny's head, Below stood back and lined Danny up for a powerful smash to the face. He let loose a roar as he fired his fist at Danny. Danny watched as Below's face suddenly changed tempo his fist stopped in mid air, just barely touching his face. Danny couldn't believe his eyes as he watched what looked like a forearm materialized around Below's arm, from out of nowhere. Below's face changed several different shades of colors as his body rose up in the air and he was thrown over the table. Greager turned to look just in time to see his partner crash to the floor on the other side of the room. He turned and was shocked by the sight of a man standing beside him. Greager threw a punch that seemed to land in mid air. The man returned a series of blows that broke Greager down to his knees. He then grabbed and sent him flying upside down into the concrete wall. The stranger grabbed Danny and threw him to the floor as a rapid discharge of 40 Caliber rounds tore through the air towards them. It was Below, he'd recovered from his flight and now he was ready for his nuts.

The sound of gun fire brought several Police personnel towards the observation room. Among the first to reach the door of the room, containing the too-way mirror, was Raft and Jackson. With Jackson standing behind him, Raft opened the door just in time to see the lights go out. Raft and Jackson drew their fire arms and tried to peek through the mirror. The room was pitch black making it impossible to see anything. In addition to the darkness, the room was silent and still, as they tried to make out what they could. Suddenly, below crashed through the too-way mirror and sailed over the heads of both Raft and Jackson. He slammed into the wall on the opposite side of the room and fell to the floor.

Raft looked at Jackson and whispered; "Cover me."

Raft opened the door and the two men rushed into the room. Armed and with the help of flashlights the two men found Greager still lying on the floor. The lights clicked on and the stranger was found kneeling beside Danny about ten feet away. The two men turned and trained their weapons on the stranger as he slowly stood up and displayed his federal credentials.

As they still maintained their weapons pointed at him, nearing him with every step, Raft ordered him to the floor.

"I am a Federal Investigator." Said the stranger.

"I don't give a damn who you are!" Said Raft.

"That's obvious." The stranger said as he helped Danny to a chair.

"I said don't move, mother fucker! Or are you deaf?!" Said Raft.

The stranger stepped into the face of Raft and said. "I've seen a lot of evidence that none of your men at this Department really care about anything but themselves! And that includes even you!"

"Now what's that supposed to mean?!" Said Raft as he and Jackson began to put away their weapons.

"Well, Raft." He said as he helped Danny to his feet.

"Where do you think you're going with him?" Said Raft.

"It's going to be a real pleasure working with you." Said the stranger as he opened the door to room, allowing the Paramedics to rush into the room and attend to Danny.

"Hey, you're not taking him anywhere and what do you mean you're going to be working with me? I don't need your help." Said Raft as he ran and jumped in front the stranger and Paramedic's path.

The stranger stopped and with an angry expression upon his face said; "Look Raft, so far you guys have done a lot to piss me off. Let's not make it any worse. But I'll be back tomorrow at nine A.M. When, I've had time enough to calm down."

As the two the Paramedics wheeled Danny past everyone on their way out, both the Stranger and Danny were met with strange looks. The stranger watched as Danny was loaded into the ambulance. Once they had secured him he joined him inside. As the Paramedics shut the doors and drove away, they were watched by everyone. During the ride Danny occasionally looked up at the stranger. He was an average sized man of normal build. He had a brown complexion and his hair was cut short. He sat with his eyes closed and didn't look at Danny. His face held an intense look of determination on it, as if there were one hundred thousand and one things he was mentally simultaneously concentrating on. In spite of his facial expression, he seemed to have a kind face. He didn't look like he smoked or anything, but of course who can tell. Still Danny had an odd feeling about him. Something familiar that he couldn't quite put his hand on. It would have been frustrating if it wasn't for such a calming feeling that he got from the man's presences. The Ambulance pulled into the emergency room entrance at Soft Stone General Hospital and as the Paramedics opened the doors, Danny saw his Mother and Uncle Aaron standing outside the back doors. With tears running down her face, his mother hugged Danny tightly as the Paramedics sat Danny's gurney down.

At first she wanted to hold him forever, but Uncle Aaron touched her on the shoulder and said; "Let's let them get him inside." As the Paramedics lifted Danny's gurney and took him inside he thought that he would never see this place or any other ever again. The stranger got out of the Ambulance and saw that Danny was now being guarded by both his mom and Uncle Aaron. The stranger turned and trailed them as they all went inside. Once they disappeared into the Emergency room he stopped and let them go.

Uncle Aaron started to make sure that no one was going to harm his nephew ever again his mom said; "No, no no. I want him to have a thorough examination and call his therapist Dr. Suzan Hcrion, and tell her that I want her to get down here and see him as soon as possible."

Uncle Aaron said;. "Where did he go?"

"He's probably still outside. He'll be in shortly." Said Lillian.

Once mom got started helping the nurses to get me undressed, Uncle Aaron went outside to see where the stranger was. Uncle Aaron came back and said; "He's gone."

Mom looked at him and gave him one of her angry looks. She gives you one of those looks when she secretly wants to kill you, but refuse to say so.

The nurses got me undressed and helped me back into bed. After a full batter of tests were done, plus the visit from my therapist Susan, mom slept next to me in bed as Uncle Aaron slept in a chair on the other side. The two of them wanted to be right there with me. They just didn't want me to be alone and I didn't want to be alone either. As I slept I heard something out in the hallway. I started thinking about her and wondered if she would be there this time. If she would be hurting or suffering, maybe I could stop him. Maybe this time I could finally stop him from taking her into the darkness; if she is still alive. I sat up and slipped out from under mom's hand. I stepped out into the hallway and stopped at the closet to pick up his favorite baseball bat. It was a Louie Ville Slugger, left to me by my own father. My mother brought it from St. Louis Missouri when I was just a little boy. Danny carried the large ended bat as he walked down the hallway. He jumped out into the hallway ready to do battle. A shadow went past him and he swung breaking his mother's lamp. Danny started thinking that if this isn't a dream; he is in a lot of trouble.

"Boy, go back to bed." A voice said to Danny, from out of nowhere.

The voice sounded familiar, it was the stranger who rescued him from the Police Station yesterday.

"Hey, what are you doing here?" Danny said.

"Daniel, go back to bed." The stranger said.

"Hey, who are you?" Said Danny.

"What dose it matter?" Said the stranger.

"That's what My Mom always says." Said Danny.

"I can't help you with that." Said the stranger.

"Yeah, she says that a lot too. Do you know my Mom?" Asked Danny.

"There was a time when all I had to do was just fly you around like an air plane and you always went right to sleep." Said the stranger.

Danny was frozen; He couldn't believe the stranger's last comment. He couldn't move. Every square inch of him was stuck. He had just spoken to his Father for the first time and he didn't know how to handle it.

"Dad, why can't I see you?" Asked Danny.

"Daniel this is not the time to talk and believe me you're going to need all the strength you can get. So, do as I say and just go to bed." Said his father's voice.

Danny went back to his bed room and slipped back into his bed. He couldn't wait till morning to see him. Maybe he could help him find out what to do with his loss. Maybe he could help with a lot of things. After lying there in bed with his Mother beside him, he started thinking about his Father and his Mother and again wondered just what happened between them. Maybe he would have some of those questions answered for once and then the mystery that surrounds the events leading up to the present will be clear.

CHAPTER 16

"How in the hell can you just let a guy come in to my station and run off the suspect!" Yelled Raft.

"Well now, it looked like to me that he more or less left with your blessing!" Replied Jackson.

"I didn't give any one my blessing to do shit!" Screamed, Raft as he stood over Jackson, who was sitting in a chair.

Jackson jumped to his feet, which moved Raft backward immediately and with that he began dishing out what Raft had been giving him. Neither one noticed that they had a visitor.

"Huh." He clears his voice and the two come to a complete stop.

"Well, you said nine A.M. and it's after nine." Said Raft.

"Actually, I was here at ten till. The rest of the time has been spent waiting on you to stop dancing with this guy." He Replied.

"Where's my suspect?!" Raft yelled.

The stranger walked towards Raft and said right to his face. "If you mean the witness, he's in a hospital room over at Soft Stone Cove General. But ya know, I think the boy's mother is really wishing that you would walk into her son's hospital room. I think that she would probably regard it as Christmas time comes early."

Raft was suddenly quiet as if he was contemplating the stranger's words. The stranger walked around Raft and took a look at the Photos of the crime scene that were displayed on a bulletin board. The two men stood silent as the stranger studied each photo quickly and quietly.

He stepped back and as he stared at the entire board and whispered; "Tommy Thompson's in town."

He turned and started walking towards the door and Raft yelled; "What did you say?!"

He stopped, turned and paused, giving Raft a look, and after a moment of uncomfortable silence answered; "I have to meet with somebody."

Raft, clearly aware of what the look he received meant, this time took care to speak in a much calmer voice. "And who is that?"

"Raft, my name is Sebastian and I think I have a lead on finding out what happened, I'll be back later after I see where it takes me." Said Sebastian.

Raft replied. "O.K., but you're in our town and it's a small town. And I would appreciate it if you took one of my guys with you. Folks around here get spooked real easily."

Sebastian nodded and disappeared past the doorway. Raft looked at Jackson and said; "Get someone to go with him; I can't take the chance on a Fed getting himself killed in our neck of the woods. After all, this ain't L.A. If something happens to him, everyone from Quantico Virginia will drive up here and take up residency."

Jackson grabbed his coat and said; "No sir, I'll go with him myself."

"Suit yourself." Said Raft.

Jackson caught up with Sebastian. He was leaning on his car patiently waiting.

Jackson approached him saying; "Looks like it's me that you're stuck with."

The two men got into the car and Sebastian drove off. He began making turns cutting through the heart of town. He drove directly to a bad part of town, it was a place that every good cop in Soft Stone Cove was aware of and rarely visited. Cops who had this section of the city would never be seen driving the area until they absolutely had to. Strange things had a way of happening and it wasn't limited to just civilians. Cops had also been known to disappear. The old Chief Bernard Rensit, during his reign, declared the area off limits after so many bad things happened out there. Over time, when things died down and the old Chief later retired to Florida, the area was sold a couple of times. Sebastian, pulled through a clearing in some heavy brush. The sun seemed to stop shining all of a sudden as the two men got out of the vehicle. Jackson noticed that it was quiet, too quiet. The whole place was eerie. Sebastian looked over his shoulder at Jackson and saw that he was a little worried.

Sebastian stopped and said; "Hey look you don't have to come with me. Just take the car and leave me here. I'll walk out by myself in a while."

Jackson gave Sebastian a look and said; "Yeah right, and when something happens to you I get to draw an early pension, and live out the rest of ma days dreaming about how I let that kid's father get killed while I sat out here all nice, comfy and safe."

Sebastian smiled and disappeared into the brush. Jackson looked down at his feet for a moment and said; "Damn it!"

Jackson got around to the front of the car and started to look for a way in. A hand reached out from nowhere and snatched him into the bushes. Once on the other side he was face to face again with Sebastian.

"Thanks." Said Jackson.

"Don't mention it." Sebastian replied as he turned to walk through a small clearing.

Sebastian, approached another wall of thick brush and disappeared once again. Jackson took a deep breath and bowed his head down and tore through the brush and once again he joined Sebastian on the other side. Jackson found Sebastian staring across another clearing at several tall trees all grouped together.

"O.K. what's next?" Said Jackson.

"I'm going in there, but like I said. You don't have to come with me." Said Sebastian.

"Where's there?" Asked Jackson.

Sebastian started walking towards the trees. As the two men closed the distance between themselves and the trees. Sebastian turned and said; "It's too late to part, so just keep close and don't touch anything. Even, if it touches you first."

Jackson gave Sebastian a strange look and followed him past the first set of trees. He was relieved that he didn't have any more bushes to fight his way through, but suddenly he was joined by that feeling again. Except this time it was stronger. That feeling of eeriness he first experienced when he first got out of the car. Something told him that he would soon wish that he had taken Sebastian up on his offer to stay back at the car. Jackson found himself standing outside what looked like a large barn. The trees and the brush were so thick that when Jackson tried to see the sky he couldn't. It was pitch black like the night and as the two men stood at the door, Jackson took a closer look at the doors. He couldn't make out the color of the building, so to make sure that he wasn't imagining it he started to reach out and touch the doors.

Sebastian grabbed Jackson's arm and said; "Now, now didn't we talk about this already?"

Jackson gave Sebastian a look of ridiculousness. The doors slowly opened and the two men went inside. The floor was covered in a mixture of dirt and hay. Plus there was a horrible smell that seemed to travel around the room. The two men stood in the middle of a large room. The room was so dark it was impossible to see the walls, but still Jackson knew that they were not alone. He could see something moving underneath the dirt and hay. It traveled back and forth. Jackson tried to focus, but as he was making one of them out another rushed past him from behind. Jackson nearly leaped out of his skin and started to shout, but Sebastian quickly grabbed hold of him and covered his mouth with his hand. The scream of a door swung open and a figure of a man stood in the door way. He turned and walked back into the room.

"Look I'm sorry, but I do usually like to work alone. Your Boss wouldn't let me just leave unless I allowed him to send along one of his people to baby sit, but I promise you if you just wait here and don't make any sudden movements; nothing, I repeat, nothing will happen to you. O.K.?" Said Sebastian and then he turned and walked through the doorway of the open door.

Jackson tried to see where Sebastian went, but the outer room was just as dark as the one that he was standing in.

Sebastian walked along a path that leaded him to another room in the rear of the barn. As he stepped through the doorway into the room he noticed human bones hanging from the ceiling by twines of string they were illuminated by rays of sun that managed to force its way through. Tommy sat in the farthest corner of the room, away from the rays.

"Looks like you guys went off the reservation." Said Sebastian.

Tommy didn't reply.

"Tell me your children didn't dine on fresh meat the other night." Asked Sebastian.

"What if we did? What will you do about it?" Asked Tommy.

Sebastian turned his back and took a closer look at the hanging tarsal. The arms and one leg was missing. It was a man and he wasn't fresh. He looked like he'd been dead for several months. A familiar feeling swept over Sebastian and as he spun around he drew his gun. The muzzle of his weapon rested on Tommy's upper lip and when he backed up it left an imprint.

"Tommy, what's the problem? You have to trust me, but if you're pack is feeding on live flesh, they're going to put an end to you and you know that." Said Sebastian.

"We haven't feasted on live prey since forever and a day." Said Tommy.

"Since you and your covenant made the deal with Chief Rensit. A deal that's managed to keep peace between you and the living for quite some time." Said Sebastian.

Sebastian, now deep in thought, put his weapon away and started to stare at his feet. Tommy noticed that he was troubled and said; "Why are you so wrapped up in this? You've suffered through this before. We all have, at least those of The Professor's Kids that are left. Why does this matter so much now?"

"Tommy how's your little boy? Is he safe? Is he happy? You know, without you? Your old man, however late that he was, stood up for us." Said Sebastian.

"He's alright. My dad and mom take good care of him." Replied Tommy.

"Tommy do you see him?" Asked Sebastian.

"No. No I don't, but I know that he's O.K." Answered Tommy.

"You never go and look in on him? You never stand at his bed side and worry about him as you watch him sleeping?" Asked Sebastian.

Tommy seemed to stir about. The issue of his own child seemed to bother him more than he would admit. Sebastian realized that his own fears were actually shared by others of his small group. They had survived a horrible childhood no child should ever have to go through and now they were in fear for their own children. Each night they wake in horror to thoughts and memories of the past and now if that wasn't bad enough. The legacy of their horror may await their children.

Sebastian went and stood in the sun's rays and after a moment he looked to his side and saw Tommy standing beside him. Tommy's complexion was as white as a sheet and his eyes were a deep dark blood red.

"Man, you've got to start thinking about getting some sun and take these so when you do you won't hurt your peepers." Said Sebastian as he handed Tommy a pair of expensive Ray Ban sun glasses.

Back in the other room, Jackson was becoming irritated with watching the dirt and the hay shift around him. He started hearing strange sounds and then one stopped in front of him. It started coming closer, very slowly at first and then it stopped just short of him. It sped back the opposite direction and started all over again. Coming closer and closer again, it was tormenting Jackson. It didn't like his presence and it grew increasingly impatient for the time of his departure. It slowed down again and this time stopping just in front of him. Jackson became nervous as he watched it remain still in front of him. It burst from the ground and stood two inches from Jackson's face. It was covered in what looked like a dirt colored burlap sack. There were two cut out dark patches that served as eyes. Jackson took out a mini flashlight and shined it into the holes of the figure and could see clear through the sack. It was empty.

"If you're through making friends, it's time to go." Sebastian said standing behind Jackson.

Sebastian turned and walked away and as he exited the door Jackson hurried to catch up to him.

CHAPTER 17

"Dr. Suzan Herion is here to see Danny." A nurse said as she opened the curtains.

In she walks, stepping briskly and full of life. She is everything of chipper and as enthusiastic as she's been trained to be. She grabs a seat and sits down beside Danny's bed. After a momentary greeting of Danny's Mother and Uncle, they both leave the room.

"Hello, and how are we doing today?" She said looking at Danny's chart.

Danny nodded his response.

"Hey, what's the matter? Cat got your tongue?" She said still smiling.

She continued on to say; "It certainly looks like you've had an interesting night. Do you want to talk about anything?"

Danny wasn't really in the mood to talk to her about anything. As a matter of fact he didn't really want to see her at all. Every time he had a visit with her, all she wanted to talk about was whether or not he wanted to hurt himself or any one. That and the fact that she always wanted to keep him medicated was always a pain in his ass. He once talked to one of her other patients, while he was waiting for his appointment and she told him that Dr. Herion believes in keeping all of her patients heavily medicated. The other teen told him that Dr. Herion likes it when you're drugged. She feels that it makes it easier to control them and it allows her to conduct her case studies for the purposes of her book.

"So you don't have anything that you want to say? You're totally alright with what happened to you? You're not mad with the Soft Stone Cove Police for what they did to you? Well, do you want to at least talk about Dene Pairtree or Darla Kavanaugh? You're not mad about the Soft Stone Cove Police Department feeling that you're their best lead to finding out what happened to those two girls? Asked Dr. Herion.

Danny just nodded no to all of her questions and at the end of the last one his Mother walked back into the room and said; "Excuse me Suzan, can I talk to you outside for a moment?"

Once outside of the room Danny can see them argue from the window of his hospital room.

"I'm only trying to help him to get out of this mess." Said the Dr. Herion.

"Yeah right, by interrogating him?! I don't think so! I told you that I wanted you to make sure that he was O.K. Not forward your book career by exploiting my son!" Yelled Lillian.

Danny watched as Uncle Aaron came in and said; "Hey, Bud what's going on?"

"Nothing, I'm just watching Mom and my therapist get along." Said Danny.

Uncle Aaron looked out to see what Danny was talking about. The two women were so engaged in such a heated argument that the head Nurse walked over from a nearby nurses station and unlocked the conference room for them.

"Lillian, I'm just trying to help." Said Dr. Herion.

"O; bullshit! You were interrogating my son and I want to know why?" Said Lillian.

"I'm his therapist and I'm only trying to help him work this out for himself and everyone involved." Said Dr. Herion.

"Well, I'm not paying you to help everyone who this involves. I'm paying you to help him get through this! Said Lillian.

"How can I help Danny, if I can't ask him about what's happened?" Said Dr. Herion.

"Look, just help my son and not your book career or the damned Soft Stone Cove Police Department?!" Said Lillian.

"Now, that is unethical and not to mention unlawful. I can not divulge any information about Danny to anyone without the written permission of you and Danny." Said Dr. Herion.

"Well you know Suzan, if you think that you can leak any information about my son and get away with it, I want to assure you that not only will I have your license, but I'll also have your ass charged and that's in addition to financially ruining you. I damned guarantee it!" Lillian said in a quiet stern low voice.

Danny and Uncle Aaron watched as Dr. Herion burst from the conference room door. She took a moment to straighten her suit and then she continued down the hallway.

"Wonder who won?" Said Uncle Aaron

Just then Lillian calmly walked out of door of the conference room. She placed her hands on her hips as she watched Dr. Herion stepped on to the elevator. After the elevator doors closed, Lillian started walking towards the Danny's hospital room.

They both looked at each other and said; "I knew it."

They scrambled to look busy before she walked into the room. She walked into the room and looked at the both of them. She grabbed hold of the phone and called Marsha at the office.

No one was there so she left a message. "Marsha, it's the middle of the day of a work week and I'm talking to your message service. Why aren't you there? You'd better not be shopping. Call me when you get this." Said Lillian.

"So, have you heard from him?" Said Uncle Aaron.

Lillian didn't say anything, but after a pause she finally shook her head no. Uncle Aaron then said; "Well maybe we ought to go into the little conference room and chat about this too."

Lillian laughed and said. "I don't think so."

"Well, it's going to happen sometime and we were just talking about this just the other day. I mean the guy is finally here in Soft Stone Cove. Hey, what are the odds!" Uncle Aaron said as he raided his voice.

Lillian knew that, for once, Uncle Aaron finally had her over a barrel. The two of them had played this game over and over since childhood. Their parents would tell you that they were really something when they were kids. They fought about everything. The weather, her boyfriends, his girlfriends and believe it or not they once even argued over which one of their own Mother's nipples had the best milk!

"When are you guys going to stop arguing about my Dad?" Said Danny.

The silence was so loud you couldn't have heard an elephant getting an enema with a tube the size of Texas. After a moment or two passed, Lillian looked over at Uncle Aaron, who had the same look of astonishment on his face as she did. He was staring at Danny like he had two heads. Uncle Aaron then looked over at Lillian and when their eyes met he walked across the room and right out the door.

Lillian looked at the empty doorway and said. "Typical, little brother, you're always there when I need you."

Danny said; "O.K. I'm ready."

CHAPTER 18

The wall of water was hot and steaming as Sebastian dove underneath the shower head first. The water seared his back as it ran free down his body. Thoughts of the earlier part of his day with Jackson were troubling him as he turned from one side of the shower to the other. He thinks that even though Tommy isn't involved, some of the others have to be, it only makes sense that way. He'll try and build up a following; it's the only way that he'll get stronger. It's the only way that he'll have what he wants.

He is done showering and he opens the door he finds a women standing in front of him with a pistol. Together with the gun, she was trembling like she was in the middle of an earthquake. At the rate that her body was shaking he started thinking that if the gun went off the round would hit him or herself. She was terrified of him and of something else.

Sebastian said. "O.K. If you want my wallet it's in the other room."

She didn't respond, except that she shook even more. He noticed that the mere sound of his voice sent waves of fear through her. He realized that if he made any sudden movements it would cause her trembling hand to constrict and discharge a round.

"You know, this isn't going to get us anywhere." Sebastian said.

Still she didn't respond in any way.

"Look, I'm going to reach for a towel. Now if you want to shoot me on purpose then this is your opportunity to do so." Said Sebastian.

He reached out his hand and took a towel off the rack. As he started to dry his head and then the rest of his body, he stepped out of the shower and went into the outer bedroom. She watched as he began to get dressed. He moved slowly so that he didn't alarm her and once he was finished, he sat down and crossed his legs.

"Please have a seat." Sebastian said.

She didn't move. Her face turned angry and the gun started to tremble less. She seemed to be more focused on him now or was she just ready for him to make a move on her.

"Look, we're going to have to develop some form of communication because I can't and won't stay in this room all my life. I don't have enough money to do that. So, let's talk about what's bothering you." Said Sebastian.

"He said that you were dangerous, that you were the reason for the murders." She said as she began to tremble more violently.

"Who said that I'm dangerous?" Asked Sebastian.

Her gun hand started shaking again and her eyes let go of two large tears. As they rolled off her cheeks, she began to break down. It looked as though she had been through some sort of ordeal. Her clothing was clean, but her hands were dirty. Her nails looked like she had recently clawed her way out of somewhere. Her shoes looked like her hands.

"You know, let's not even talk about him right now. Let's, just talk about each other. So, hi. Hi ya doing? I'm new in town. Do you come here often?" Sebastian said with a smile on his face.

For a moment she exposed a smirk, but she lost it as soon as it appeared. He saw that she was broken. The kinda broken that comes from being exposed to something horrific.

"Look, something bad happened and it happened to you. I'd like to help but I can't unless you trust me. I can see that you're in pain and I want to give you the assurance that everything is going to be alright." Sebastian spoke in a calm voice.

She became increasingly tired, she leaned forward as her head fell backward and her eyes rolled. Sebastian caught her before she hit the floor. He turned to watch as the weapon fell from her hand. Holding her in one arm he reached out and also recovered the gun before it could hit the floor. He could feel her bones coming through her clothing. She was starving and exhausted. There was a knock at the door. He picked her up and carried her over to the bed. After taking off her shoes, he covered her up and went to answer the door.

He took a look in the peep hole and whispered in a loud voice. "Shit!"

He turned and leaned with his back up against the door and thought for a moment that maybe he could pretend that he wasn't in. There it was again the knock, but this time it was harder, longer and more determined.

Sebastian whipped the door open and said; "Yeah, what can I do for you?"

"Well hot damn, it's nice to see you too! Did I interrupt you from doing something?!" Said Lillian.

Sebastian couldn't believe it. What are the chances that this could happen twice in one life time? The first time was planned, but this time. This time she was here and everything was wrong, but he had to talk to her. It was unavoidable.

"Well can I come in or not?!" Lillian said sharply.

"I'm sorry, but the place is a mess." Said Sebastian.

"That's not what Vera says." Replied Lillian.

"Who's Vera?" Asked Sebastian.

"She's the maid who cleaned your room." Answered Lillian.

"How do you know that?" Asked Sebastian.

"Because, we were both in the same troop as Girl Scouts." Answered Lillian.

"Small world, huh?" Said Sebastian.

"Uh hum." Replied Lillian as she nodded.

"Well, that was earlier and now the place has that nice homey look that I'm used to." Said Sebastian.

"I can't believe it. You're not going to let me in." Said Lillian.

The two exchanged looks and she turned and walked away. He watched her as she walked down the hallway. He knew that she was hurt. All he could think of was that it was happening again, bad things were being done for the right reason.

He started thinking to himself. Before this is over there's going to be a lot of unnecessary bloodshed, both good and bad. I just don't have the stamina for this type of deception, I never did. I can't go after her, not right now. Not with so much at stake.

Sebastian closed the door and went back inside. He looked in on her and found an empty bed. He started a visual sweep of the room and found no one. Suddenly it struck him; He kneeled down and looked up under the bed. Clutching her firearm, she was lying underneath his bed sound asleep.

He shook his head and whispered. "Well what do ya know."

CHAPTER 19

"Well, what you guys turn up?" Asked Raft as he walked along the hallway with Jackson.

"All we turned up was nothing." Answered Jackson.

"You mean to tell me that after all that time spent out in Nomad's Land, that's all you guys came up with was nothing?" Said Raft.

"No I'm not saying that." Said Jackson.

Raft stopped him and said; "Jackson, did you guys turn up yesterday or not? I mean, I need to know. I mean, don't start liking this guy and start keeping secrets."

Jackson pissed at the insult, said. "I'm not picking sides. I'm not withholding information either. All I'm doing is trying to get to the bottom of this mess."

"Hey, I'm not saying that you're withholding anything. All I'm saying is know who pays your salary." Said Raft.

"I understand. You're threatening me and if you think that I'm going to take that then you've got another thing coming." Replied Jackson.

"Hey, Lieutenant. I'm not trying to say anything bad. I'm just talking here. You know, just giving you a little friendly advice." Said Raft.

"Yeah, well thank you for caring." Jackson said as he walked away.

Raft opened the door to his office and found his chair occupied. He walked in and slammed the door saying. "Hey, are ya comfortable?!"

"Yes, thank you for asking." He said.

"Good, remove yourself from my chair." Said Raft.

The stranger leaned back in the chair and said; "You've got something that belongs to me."

"And what's that?" Replied Raft.

"Polezogopoulos." Said the stranger.

"And what's a Po... Pa... What you said." Asked Raft.

"Polezogopoulos, you know him by Sebastian." Replied the stranger.

"So, he lied about who he was? I knew that there was something not right about that guy. Please tell me that he's an escaped lunatic and he's to be shot on sight." Asked Raft.

"No, he's not a lunatic, but he did escape from duty in St. Louis, Missouri." Said the stranger.

"Why does this sound familiar? Wait I know. Lillian is his ex-wife, isn't she?" Asked Raft.

"It's more complicated than that. Sebastian is his first name and the two of them split after something happened in their relationship. As his superior, I had been trying to get him to face marital problems because I think that it would allow me to put an end to the murders that we are investigating. I truly think that the two aspects are linked in some kinda way. Said the stranger.

"In what way?" Asked Raft.

"Oh, they are. There's no doubt in my mind, what so ever. The murders stopped after he saved her. He saved her from what we call is a covenant." Said the stranger.

"Wait a minute. Isn't a covenant supposed to be a group of witches?" Asked Raft.

"Authentically yes, but you see St. Louis was experiencing a rash of gruesome ritualistic murders. People were disappearing from all over Missouri and neighboring states. For awhile we didn't have anything. Nothing we profiled made any sense. Until one night a college girl by the name of Penny Hilltop went missing. The girl's mother, Miss. Florence Hilltop, flooded the St. Louis Police Department and our office in Quantico Virginia. We didn't know it at the time, but Penny had fallen into a cult, but it wasn't just any cult, this was a covenant. They were leaving these horribly slain victims all over town. Penny was the turning point." Said the stranger.

"Why, what made this girl Penny so much different?" Asked Raft.

"Well as you know, we can profile these guys over and over until we're blue in the face, because some times, with good hard detective work, we get closer and closer to catching them and sometimes they just make a mistake. This time, at least we think, this group was so unique and they had been so successful. The covenant had been too confident and finally made a mistake. Penny was the mistake. They took her back to her dorm and discovered that she had a roommate. A roommate that they also kidnapped. The roommate was Lillian." Said the stranger.

"So that's how they met. Tell me where does the witch stuff fit in?" Asked Raft.

"I don't know. The covenant seems to be operating upon the premise that they think they are a bunch of witches." Said the stranger.

"What do you think?" Asked Raft.

"About what?" Said the stranger.

"Do you think they're a bunch of witches?" Asked Raft.

"Why would I?" Said the stranger.

"I don't know. I was just fucking with you." Said Raft as he laughed.

The stranger didn't say a word. His face was like stone as he got up and walked around to the front of Raft's desk. He leans back against the desk and says. "You know, in our profession, usually one's need to be funny is an attempt to hide his fear of guilt."

"No shit! Well, in that case you'll be happy to know that I sleep like a baby." Said Raft as he makes his way around the desk and reclaims his throne with a smile.

The stranger stands and says; "Well I'll let you get back to your busy schedule."

"Hey not so fast. You know people really don't like identifying themselves and I mean at all." Said Raft.

"What are you talking about?" Asked the stranger.

"I need some identification. Something to prove who you are." Said Raft.

The stranger walked back to the desk and displayed his photo identification and said; "Now what's the second thing."

"O.K. is it Shepard?" Asked Raft.

Shepard nodded yes.

"Do you want to know where your boy is?" Asked Raft.

Shepard said as he opened the door and walked out. "That's alright. I've always known where he was."

CHAPTER 20

"Help me! Help me! Danny help! Danny, don't you hear me? Its Darla, can't you hear me!" Said Darla.

Danny finds himself standing in the center of Madelyn's Food and Gas Mart. It was dark as he walked towards the men's restroom. He reached for the handle of the door, but stopped. He started thinking to himself. Where is Dene? How come I don't hear her voice?

Danny said; "Dene, are you in there?"

There was silence.

"Darla are you alright?" Said Danny.

"Danny let me out. Danny I can't get out. Please let me out!" Said Darla.

Danny grabbed hold of the door knob, but he was still reluctant to turn it. A bad feeling came over him and he let go and stepped back.

"What's the matter Danny? Just open the door and let me out. I want to get out of here." Said Darla.

The door started to shake and Danny turned and started walking towards the door. As he made his way down the isles, he could hear her calling to him.

Danny, Danny come back and help me! The voice started to change as the tone started to get heavier and heavier.

The floor started to move sending the entire store towards the men's rest room door. By then Danny was running for the exit, but it was impossible to reach. The men's rest room door turned into a vacuum. Danny could see things fly through the air as he ran faster to reach the exit. The floor started to rise, the exit was harder and harder to reach.

He looked at the glass doors as his body lay in a mud like linoleum floor. His hands continued to disappear as they sank with each attempt to claw his way up to the exit.

Danny turned his head and said. "Darla, is Dene with you?"

With that everything suddenly came to a halt.

"Danny, help me." Said Darla.

"What do you want me to do?" Said Danny.

"You have to open the door, Danny. It's the only way." Answered Darla.

Danny climbed down and approached the men's restroom door and said; "Darla, is Dene in there with you too?"

"Danny, just open the door. That's all you have to do." Said Darla.

"If I open this door what will happen? Will you be free?" Asked Danny.

"Yes, Danny. Oh, yes. I'll finally be free. Free to be out there with you. Free to be with the rest of the world. Free like I've always wanted." Said Darla.

"What's it like in there?" Asked Danny.

"It's horrible. It's dark all the time and I'm so afraid. There's no one to talk to and I'm so, so lonely." Answered Darla.

"So how long have you been in there?" Asked Danny.

"It's been ages. Ages, since I've had the light of the moon upon my face. Ages since I've felt the fresh breath of the innocent. I so want that. I so need that again to be whole." Said Darla.

"Why can't you open the door yourself?" Said Danny.

"Because I'm weak and I'm hurt. I can't open the door." Said Darla.

Danny had already figured out that this was not Darla. He set his sites on trying to learn as much as he possibly could. He started looking around the door. It was normal in every aspect except one. There was a strange bright glow in between all the sides of the door.

"How did you get in this spot? Who put you in there?" Asked Danny.

There was a pause and then she answered; "I don't know what happened. I just woke up here and I've been trapped every since with no way out. At least until you came along."

"What happened here? What happened to Dene and Darla?" Asked Danny.

Again there was a pause and then the voice said; "Danny, it's important that you hear me. I've got to get out of here and you have to help me."

"Why?" Asked Danny.

The door buckled as something hit it hard from inside. Again and again with each and every blow the door took on a new shape. Suddenly the pounding come to a complete stop.

"If you don't, you'll never know where your girlfriend is." Said the voice.

"I thought you said that you were in there alone?" Said Danny.

"I want you to turn the door knob and let me out!" Said the voice.

Danny stood on the opposite side of the door. He started looking at the door as it started to swell. It suddenly crystallized and turned from grey to a murky blue color. As Danny stared into the door, it was like looking into ocean water. He sat down in front of the door and continued to stare into it. He watched as it fluctuated in front of his eyes. A small black speck appeared in the center of his view.

"You know Danny, I knew your father. He was as inquisitive as you. Except for your color, you are the spitting image of him. Yes, I can tell that we are going to be close. Real close, closer than me and your father ever were." Said the voice.

While talking Danny got to his feet and started to look around for a way out. The store was still inverted. He could see the exit high up above him out of his reach. Behind him the dot had grown into a smaller dark figure.

"Your father was one of my best pupils. He far exceeded all of my hopes and dreams. He reached a level of awareness that none of the others could have achieved. Though some were very talented, Sebastian was truly gifted." Said the voice.

Danny started looking at the isles; he wondered how sturdy they were. Since the lights were off, it was difficult to see if the railings went as far as the exit.

"I'll bet that your Mother still doesn't have a clue as to who your farther really is. After all, he's a mystery to even himself. How could he even hope to tell her when he doesn't even know himself. I created him and I made him the indescribable thing that he is. It's a pity that he's wasting himself. The constant thought of what he's doing with the incredible gift that I've given him irritates me to no end!" Said the voice.

At the rise of his voice, a large slam was heard. Danny turned to see what it was and looked at the door. The figure was blackish blue. It was so large it filled up the entire door. Danny stood like a child looking at something the size of a whale through some thick glass at sea world. It moved back and forth as it studied Danny.

Still speaking in Darla's voice it said; "Do you find me hideous?"

Danny was speechless at the site of it. No matter how much he tried to, he still couldn't figure out how to describe it. It had three tails and red hair that ran clear down its back. Its face looked to be smooth with black freckles and two sets of nostrils that sat on top of each other. The two nostrils worked simultaneously, one breathing while the other was closed. Its eyes were red and seemed to pierce right through him.

"I asked you a question Danny and you did not answer me, why?" It said as it came to a complete stop.

Looking at its red beard and full breast, he wondered why it continued to sound like Darla. He couldn't help but be frozen, lock in place.

Finally Danny said; "I'm sorry for staring. I know it's impolite and I apologize."

It said nothing. He didn't know whether it was shocked or merely contemplating its next question.

"No, I'm serious. It was wrong of me to stare and if I upset you or made you feel uncomfortable in any way please forgive me." Said Danny.

"Holy shit!" It responded.

"Excuse me?" Said Danny.

It paused for moment and said; "Give me a break, kid. I know that you find me repulsive and a torment to look upon."

"Why would I? You can't help what you look like." Said Danny.

"Ahh, You're so sweet. I could just eat you up like that." It said as it cracked its tails like three large bull whips with a smile. The sound was similar to thunder setting off.

"What did you want from me?" Asked Danny.

"Nothing, I just wanted to meet you. I have spent a lot of time watching you watching him." It answered him as it continued to maintain eye contact.

"You've been watching me watching who?" Asked Danny.

"I've been watching you, watch him who creates." It said.

"You mean the guy who's in my dreams?" Asked Danny.

"The one who creates his masterpieces by using your sleepy time as his canvas." It said as it waited for him to respond.

"Where are you when he's here?" Asked Danny.

"Oh, I'm always around somewhere. I pretty much see hear and see everything." It answered.

"It's not right, what he does. He's hurting people." Said Danny.

"Well actually, he only prefers female subjects for his work. It's just a thing that he's going through. Who knows maybe one day he'll decide to go find something else to play with." It said as the expression on its face seemed to be reflecting great sorrow.

"What do you mean, maybe he'll go do something else some day? He's hurting people." Argued Danny.

"Hey, kid that's what he does and this is life. And in life people get hurt. No, what am I saying. I meant, dead." It said.

"But why does it have to be this way? It makes no sense. No sense at all." Danny argued again.

"Kid, it's alright. Everything dies. Why shouldn't they. It's the cycle of life." It replied.

"What's the cycle? You mean it's the cycle to cut down, torment and let's not forget torture and execute innocent human life!" Argued Danny.

"Well, exactly! How else do you suppose it's done?" It replied as it laughed, displaying two sets of fangs. Each set sharper and more terrifying than the other.

"I see nothing funny about this." Said Danny.

"Hey, mellow out, kid. Remember, you guy's lives are short enough as it is, so you really shouldn't dwell on such things. All it'll do is just upset you." It said with a look of concern, but then a smirk appeared.

"You delight in this misery?" Danny said as tears rolled down his face.

He knew that it would not give him any information. Its only purpose in being here was to feel him out. He turned and started to climb the racks.

As he started to leave her sight, it said; "O, come on. Don't go away mad. Don't be like that."

As he got closer to the exit he could feel himself start to wake. He heard it say; "You know, you're just like your father. No sense of humor. None, at all."

Danny woke up to see his Uncle Aaron sitting in a hospital chair next to his bed. As Danny started to sit up in bed, his Uncle Aaron woke and out of reflex said. "You O.K. Bud?"

"Yeah, I'm alright." Answered Danny.

"Your Mom went to work, but later she'll be back to pick us up to go home." Said Uncle Aaron.

"Did she go see my dad?" Asked Danny.

"Yeah, but things didn't go as well as we hoped. But don't you worry about it. We're happy that he helped as much as he did. We'll get through this as best as we can and it will be O.K."

CHAPTER 21

"O.K. It's time for you to come out from under my bed." Said Sebastian.

She wouldn't move. She just looked at him with that same blank look on her face. She had been there all night and he slept in the chair in the other room. Through the night, he checked on her almost every hour to insure her safety. She slowly crept out from under the bed and slowly got to her feet.

"Come with me." Sebastian said as he walked into the other room.

She entered the room and saw a large cart in the center of the room. Sebastian uncovered the cart, revealing an array of breakfast food.

He sat down and said. "Hey grab a seat, I'm buying. Please join enjoy."

Stunned, she stood hesitating to sit down. She hadn't eaten since her ordeal, weeks ago and she was very hungry.

"No?" Sebastian said, as he took his time spreading butter on top of his pancakes.

She still didn't move, but he could hear her stomach growling from across the room.

"Oh, well. I guess I'm dining alone. Actually, I'm pretty used to it nowadays. Eating alone, that is. But it's O.K." Sebastian said as he slowly poured syrup all over his pancakes.

Sebastian picked up the newspaper and after opening it wide he started reading. She stood there listening to him as he began to eat and continue to read his paper.

"Uhmm humm, the bacon and the sausage is really good." Sebastian said as he heard her take a seat and began eating.

"Let me get that coffee for ya." Sebastian said as he reached across the table and filled her cup.

Once she was settled, Sebastian got up and took a shower. After he was dressed he walked back into the room and as he opened the door he turned and said; "O.K. kitten, Daddy has a little work to do. So, if you want anything else just charge it to the room. I'll be back latter, O.K.?"

As Sebastian left he saw a maid in the hallway on his way to the elevator. He smiled and said. "Hi Vera, do me a favor and don't clean my room."

Sebastian stepped onto the elevator and smiled again as the doors closed. As he walked through the lobby he could feel a familiar pair of eyes watching him.

Lillian uses a pass key and opens the door. She walks in and closes the door behind her. Across the room she could see a laptop computer on the desk. She pulled up a chair and as she turned it on, she took off her coat and made herself comfortable. The system opened up and displayed a section for the password. She sat back in the chair and started thinking about what it could be.

"Hello Lucille, what's your magic password?" Said Lillian.

She entered the name Lucille, but Lucille's computer screen displayed the words invalid password. She entered the names Danny, Daniel, Lillian, Baby boy and Pimp Daddy, but all came back password invalid.

"Damn it!" She screamed as she shot up from her chair in anger. She started stamping her feet as she began to pace back and forth.

She noticed the dining cart in the middle of the room. She walked over to the cart to study it more closely. As she looked over the two empty plates, she couldn't believe that she didn't see this when she first came in. She started thinking to herself that she did see Sebastian leave the hotel room, but she didn't see anyone else leave with him.

Lillian heard the shower running and said; "Well let's go get acquainted."

Lillian walked up to the bathroom door. She placed her hand on the doorknob and slowly and quietly turned it. As she waited for the knob to stop turning she could see steam coming from underneath the door.

Lillian pushed the door open just enough to peep inside. The room was full of steam and it was impossible to see who was in the shower. She slowly entered and crept up to the curtain. The steam was thicker and more intense over there. As she reached up to grab hold of the shower curtain a hand snatches her by the hair. She lets out a scream and turns to see the strange woman who spent the night.

"What the hell are you doing?!" Yelled Lillian, as she turned and looked at the stranger.

The stranger doesn't answer her. Instead she stands with her eyes trained on the shower curtain.

"Don't put your fucking hands on me! You hear me?! Don't you ever put your hands on me ever, again!" Yells Lillian.

The stranger still ignores her and continues to stare intensely at the shower. Lillian yells again; "Hey, I'm talking to you don't you hear me?!"

"Well I hear you." Said a voice from the shower.

Lillian froze, she started thinking to herself. That voice sounds familiar. She thought that she would never hear that voice ever again. Not since St. Louis Missouri. Not since she left. It can't be. No, not here. It can't be. It's the voice.

The room explodes as rounds tear through the shower curtain. The two women stood quietly waiting on some kind of response. Blood started to trickle upward from the bullet holes in the shower curtain and onto the ceiling. The strange woman started to reach for the curtain, but Lillian grabs hold of her hand.

"Ahh, you girls are no fun and Lillian it's been a long time. Tell me are you ready to pick up where we left off?" Said the voice.

"You go to hell!" Said Lillian.

"I'm back and I'm ready to take you now. So I truly hope that you're ready to go this time. If memory serves me right, you were quite the unwilling subject before. So, I'm looking forward to finally getting started this time." Answered the voice.

Lillian motioned to the strange woman to back out of the bathroom. The two women moved slowly towards the doorway of the bathroom. Blood started to drip from above. The two of them looked up and saw the entire ceiling covered with blood. It started to swirl and then whorl. The two watched as the blood began to separate and finally formed a large face.

It smiled and said; "Ladies where are you going? Stay for a while."

The two ran out of the bathroom and slammed the bathroom door. They both stood on the other side of the door, struggling to hold it closed. They could feel him trying to open the door from the other side. The two of them continued to hold on to the door knob as he pulled against them. At one point he opened the door wide enough and a surge of blood gushed out into the face of the strange woman. Lillian turned and grabbed her by the hand and ran towards the door of the hotel room. It burst out of the bathroom door. In one ball of blood, he quickly forms into another figure and starts heading for them. The strange woman reached the door of the hotel room. She grabbed the doorknob and the door wouldn't open. As it rushed towards them, Lillian grabbed hold of the cart and turned it on its side. Using the flat surface, she ran and slammed into him knocking him backwards. As it started to reform itself the two women were still struggling to open the door. Suddenly the door opened and both of them knocked over Vera, the maid. The three women looked at the figure as it came for them again. They got to their feet and started running for the elevator. It burst into the hallway and slammed against the opposite wall.

"It's so, so hard to get good help these days." It said as it began walking towards them.

Lillian kept pushing the elevator button. Vera ran for the exit and he was upon her before she could reach the door. He placed his hand over her face and the mass grew to cover her entire head. Vera tried to scream, to the other two women, her head looked like it was in a large blood red ball of blood. Lillian ran and grabbed hold of a lamp and threw it into what she figured was his head. He slapped the lamp away. The lamp was still plugged in and it sent a current that shocked him, as it burst into pieces. He let out a scream and as the voltage surged through him, he looked like he started to take on a more significant human form. Bing went the sound of the elevator door and a roar of thunder echoed through the entire hotel as a series of holes formed in his body. More of him started to take on the size shape and color a man as Sebastian ejected one clip and replaced it with another one. Fire, smoke and thunder filled the hallway as Sebastian unloaded his weapon as he continued walking towards him. Sebastian emptied his weapon into its face, causing it to release Vera. She fell to the floor and it stood there in shaking.

"No! Not yet!" It said as it crystallized again and turned dissolved down into an air vent.

Sebastian looked at Vera as she lay on the floor choking and coughing up blood. She was also bleeding from her eyes, ears and nose. He could see the blood vessels bulging in her face.

Sebastian looked at Lillian and said as he pressed the elevator button. "I thought I told you to go home?"

The elevator door opens and as he steps on Lillian yells. "Where the hell are you going?!"

"To get something to eat, if you really have to know." Sebastian said as he put his weapon away.

"What about what just happened?!" Asked Lillian.

"What just happened?" Asked Sebastian.

The doors of the elevator started to close and she stopped them saying; "You can't just leave us here!"

"Why, are you guys' hungry too?" Asked Sebastian.

Lillian held the door open while the stranger helped Vera off the floor and into the elevator.

As the elevator doors closed Sebastian said; "O.K. but if you expect me to pay, we had better go somewhere really really cheap."

CHAPTER 22

In the car they arrive at Soft Stone Cove General. Vera was admitted for third degree burns and they waited to see what the doctors have to say.

The strange woman and Lillian watch Sebastian as he talks on the phone at the nurse's station. The strange woman noticed the strong look of emotion on Lillian's face.

She asked; "You're still in love with him aren't you?"

"Still, what do you mean by still?" Lillian said as she continued to watch Sebastian.

She asked; "You're his wife, aren't you?"

"Ex-wife." Lillian quickly corrected her.

"Yeah, right." She replied.

"Hey, who are you?" Lillian asked.

"My name is Helen Saunders and up until I got involved with this nightmare I was a noisy reporter with a roommate. Now, I wish I never learned anything about any of this." Said Helen.

"You're that reporter who's been missing. They've been running alerts for you all over the local network TV news stations." Said Lillian.

"Yeah, I saw that in the lobby. Why is it the first time I get a big story that damn near gets me killed twice, they go and show the ugliest old photo they can find?" Asked Helen.

"Yeah, it did look pretty bad." Said Lillian.

"Hey, thanks. I had just broken up with my boyfriend and needless to say I had just gotten my first big job at the Soft Stone Cove Dispatch. They just had to have a photo and they wouldn't allow me to give them one." Said Helen.

Lillian suddenly drew a serious face and asked; "Why, were you in Sebastian's hotel room?"

Amused, by Lillian's attempt to be direct and get to the bottom of things between her ex-husband and Helen, she responded in the same manner and answered; "It's strictly a matter of life and death."

Lillian caught on to Helen's mimic of her facial expression and lightened up and said; "O.K., But I still need to know."

Helen thought for a moment and looked at Lillian. She repositioned herself in the chair and as her face lost all expression, she said; "Back some time ago an insane asshole wanted to prove to his colleagues and the rest of the world, that he was a genius. So like many he dabbled in a bunch of different forbidden ancient cultures that were none of his business and tried to create a group of supernatural beings that would serve only him."

"Who was he?" Asked Lillian.

"His name was Professor Theodore Hurston Grant and like all other highly motivated slugs he found a way to get what he wanted. He made a deal with a demon to insure his success and in return he agreed to wreak as much havoc as he possibly could upon the world. Tipping the scales in Satan's favor, the demon counseled the professor on what kind of a group would best suit their needs. Since the demon instructed the professor to gather subjects who would be easy to handle like lab rats, but possessed a high superior intellect. The professor, under the demon's guidance, started collecting those who would promote the least resistance to their training. Together the two of them handpicked each and every subject." Said Helen.

"Who?" Asked Lillian.

Just then Danny and Uncle Aaron walked into the waiting room. Along with them were Mr. Lesko and his Father, they had been worried about Danny and had come to check on his safety and well being. The four of them all picked up the serious conversation that was taking place between Lillian and Helen and decided to sit and not interrupt.

"The professor kidnapped large groups of children." Said Helen.

"Children?!" Asked Lillian.

"Yeah, children with high I.Q.'s. The professor searched for them using his resources and connections with colleges and internet school systems. And then one by one they disappeared." Answered Helen.

"How's that possible?" Asked Lillian.

"You're kidding, right? Kids disappear every day in America." Said Helen.

Lillian shocked at Helen's cavalier attitude said; "Well, it's obvious that you don't have any children. Just get to the part of why you were in Sebastian's hotel room."

"Subject #1789." Helen answered.

"Subject #1789? Who's Subject #1789?" Asked Lillian.

"After countless efforts of trial and error, the two of them had finally comprised a group of children that were both talented and unique in every way. Everything was going their way or so the professor thought. The professor made two mistakes. One cost him his life's dream and the other cost him his life." Said Helen.

"How's that?" Asked Lillian.

"Well the first mistake the professor made was in trusting a demon to live up to its part of the bargain. From the beginning the demon had its own agenda. It secretly groomed the children, behind the professor's back. But by the time the professor met his end, they both discovered a shocking revelation." Said Helen.

Agitated, Lillian said; "Who is Subject #1789!"

"Subject #1789, was a child whom neither demon nor the professor were aware of until it was too late. They discovered that the child possibly had advanced supernatural abilities already and in spite of the child's young age, they also discovered that it may have been aware of its abilities before being kidnapped." Answered Helen.

"How old was the child?" Asked Lillian.

"I don't know. Apparently, all the Feds have been able to find out from the professor's notes and other information that was confiscated at his home, office, classroom and at the lecture hall was that all the children went by numbers. And when they were rescued they were all given their numbers, but in Latin. The children told the Feds that

Subject #1789 had left. They searched for the child, but there was no sign of him or her." Answered Helen.

"They don't know if it was a boy or a girl. Why is that? I mean, they're the Feds don't they know everything?" Asked Lillian.

"Well they don't. The professor used several encrypted codes for at least five or six computers and his own coded languages made up of several ancient dead languages. Even after all these years, their teams are still working on deciphering the rest of the information." Answered Helen.

"Excuse me. I'm sorry to interrupt or be noisy, but you mean to tell me that they don't know what gender this child was? He may not have gotten away, maybe he's dead." Said Uncle Aaron.

Lillian said; "I'm sorry this is my little brother Aaron and that's my son Danny.

"O.K. now, how do you know all this? I mean, because it all seems too hard to believe." Asked Uncle Aaron.

"My roommate, Clorrissa had a connection inside the Intelligence section of the Bureau. They met over the internet; the source was what we called a whisperer. Sort of a deep throat kinda stuff. Except, without the darkened parking lots. And now to answer your other question, no one really knows who Subject #1789 was. The Feds interviewed the remaining children and even though they all admit that Subject #1789 does exists. They won't give any information about him or her." Answered Helen.

"What do you mean by, Clorrissa had a connection inside of the Intelligence section?" Asked Uncle Aaron.

"Several weeks ago, one night I went to the University to get information on the Professor. It's the place where the Professor met his end at the Feds hands. I went to the Professor's old classroom to get a feel for where it all happened. As I started to investigate I found a large group of satanic symbols on the wall. I was working on the theory that the Professor had an analytical procedure to his work, but the demon had to have its own way to keep track of his work as well. And when I discovered those symbols I tried to take a look at them.

That's when I ran across what I thought was a janitor with the name of Todd. He was nice and charming until he decided to show me a trick. He said watch this and stood in front of me. He walked towards me and every step he took he got shorter and shorter as he melted into the floor right in front of my eyes. I started to look around me, but he was gone. I felt something crawling up my back. I instinctively tried to shake it off, but couldn't. There was a mirror in the room, so I went over to look at what it was and saw something that looked like a huge spider. Todd's head rested on it and he winked at me. I freaked out and threw myself into a pile of stack desks to get him off me. It fell off and rolled around on its back. Once it flipped itself over; it looked at me and said; I thought we were getting along great and you had to go and do that. It started to crawl towards me and that's when I got to my feet and ran out of the room.

I was so afraid, I left my purse behind. I was so afraid, I didn't go to the office or home and after a while, when I did go home I found the door unlocked and when I went inside the apartment. I found Clorrissa's body spread from one room of our apartment to the other. I found the majority of her body in the shower." Said Helen.

"Oh, shit!" Said Mr. Lesko, his father looked at him as if to say show some back bone.

"Mom, this is Mr. Lesko and his father. They came to see if I was alright." Said Danny.

Mr. Lesko and his father got to their feet and walked over to Lillian to properly greet her.

Lillian stood up and smiled as she greeted the two men. She quickly offered them her hand, and said; "Gentlemen, my son talks about the two of you all the time. When I noticed the two of you walk in with my brother and Danny, I immediately figured out who you were. I want to thank you for coming and please, feel free to come to dinner some night. O.K.?"

The two men thanked Lillian for her invitation, but they could sense that she was not through with her conversation with Helen. So they excused themselves and went back to sit with Danny.

Lillian returned to her seat. She turned towards Helen and said; "But, this still doesn't explain why you were in Sebastian's hotel room."

Helen could see that after all the things she had told Lillian about this group. Lillian's only focus was on Helen being in her ex-husband's hotel room.

She took a deep breath and said; "Well, as I said before the professor followed certain trained procedural techniques. I mean, where else did the subject log numbers come from? So, I figured that the demon had to have a way of keeping track of his lab rats as well. Before I could get a look at all of the satanic symbols on the wall in the back of the classroom. I did at least have enough time to look at the entire arrangement and see which symbols were set in significant positions. I made a mental note of one particular one because it was set off by itself outside the group. After I made my escape from Todd, I searched the internet and found the same symbols. But they were so ancient; I couldn't make head or tail of them."

"What were you doing in Sebastian's room?!" Yelled Lillian.

"I found out where he was staying and went there. He was taking a shower when I got there and I waited for him to come out. When he opened the shower curtain I held a gun on him and I checked him." Said Helen.

Lillian sprang to her feet and walked over to the window. She started staring out of the window. Uncle Aaron whispered to Danny and the others; "I got a feeling that we should get out of here and leave these women some privacy."

Gustavo jumped to his feet and as he started to walk he noticed that his son hadn't moved. He stopped and said; "Hey, act like I raised you with good sense and move your butt."

After the men cleared the room, Uncle Aaron who was the last to leave shut the door behind them.

Helen, feeling a little nervous said. "Hey, nothing happened and when I spent the night he slept in the chair as I slept underneath the bed. Which was pretty good because after what I've been through I hadn't been able to sleep. But what am I talking about, it shouldn't matter anyway, because, you guys are divorced."

"Oh, so you were there when I stopped by to see him last night?" Asked Lillian.

"Well yeah, but by then I was already sound asleep." Answered Helen.

"Oh, yeah?" Asked Lillian.

Danny noticed Sebastian at the nurse's station and he took a deep breath and approached him. He stood behind him, filled with fear and nervousness. He watched the back of his Father's head as he continued his phone conversation.

Suddenly he heard his father say; "Can you hold on a moment? Thank you."

Sebastian put the phone down and turned and said; "Hello, Daniel. How are you feeling?"

Danny said; "I'm fine and how are you?"

"Oh, I'm O.K." Answered Sebastian.

Danny couldn't take his eyes off his father. It was like meeting some kinda celebrity. He studied him from head to toe and said; "Well I see that you're on the phone and I just wanted to say hi."

Sebastian smiled and said; "It's O.K., but I thank you anyway."

"Agent, I think this is the call that you've been waiting on. It's on line twelve." A nurse said.

Sebastian looked at her and said; "Thank you. Excuse me, O.K.?"

Danny said; "It's O.K."

Sebastian took the call and watched Danny as he walked back to Uncle Aaron and his friends. As he continued to watch Daniel he saw Lillian come out of the waiting room. He continued to watch Lillian and Daniel together, memories started to play back to him of a time when things were pleasant. When things were so nice, it was a joy to be alive. But now it seems that they have gotten more difficult again or more hellish or ghoulish. He just wanted to spare them, but now all his years of sacrifice have been for nothing. Hell has found him after all. He hangs up the phone and lays his head down on the counter. A familiar feeling falls over him and he turns to see Lillian standing behind him.

"I would like to talk to you, Mr. Sebastian when you get the opportunity. Please, sir." Lillian said as her voice quivered with emotion.

"Oh, you don't have to be so formal." Said Sebastian.

"Oh, really?" Asked Lillian.

"Yeah, just a simple. A, you worm, come with me. Would, more than suffice." Sebastian said as he walked towards the elevator doors.

"Now where are you going?" Asked Lillian.

"I told you, I'm hungry." Said Sebastian, as he pressed the button.

"Well, that's good. Seeing as how we're all going home, you're just in time for dinner." Said Lillian.

"Oh, really. What are you guys having?" Asked Sebastian.

"Stuck pig." Answered Lillian.

Bing, went the elevator bell and when the doors opened. Sebastian stepped in and said; "Lillian, as much as you are looking forward to poisoning me, I'm afraid that it's going to have to wait. At least for now."

CHAPTER 23

Sebastian walks down the hall of a Federal Institution. It is the prison equivalent of Area 51. Accompanied by Jackson the two men stopped at a check point where they turned their weapons and everything else in. As they continued down the hall, he stopped at a door.

"Now, brace yourself." Said Sebastian.

The two walked into a large blinding white room, the center of the room had an intense glow.

Sebastian said; "Don't move."

Beep Beep Boop Bop. Went the sound of a keypad located on the wall. The light died down and a strange looking bed was revealed.

"Hello, Professor." Said Sebastian as he pulled the sheet off the bed.

The bed was shaped in the form of a large steel x about four feet tall. It was eight feet wide and twelve feet long. A man's head lay on top of it, but his body looked to be sealed into the center of it. His arms and legs were exposed, but his hands and feet were incased in large balls of steel. Suddenly large sounds of pressurized locks ignited and hydraulic machinery began to move. The head of the steel x rose first and slowly moved back towards a hollow shape the x in the wall. There was a large metallic sound as the steel x came to a stop once it was completely inserted in the wall.

"I'm back." Sebastian said as he walked towards the wall.

The professor moved his head to the sound of Sebastian's voice. He couldn't really see Sebastian due to the four inch steel bands that circled his head. His eyes and mouth were incased, but he was able to move his head from side to side.

"It's been a long time, professor." Said, Sebastian.

The professor's head swung from Sebastian to Jackson.

"I would appreciate some information, please." Said, Sebastian.

The professor's head continued to stay fixed in Jackson's direction.

"Vo Comp Activate." Said Sebastian.

With that a large digitized bong sounded and echoed throughout the room. Sebastian could feel Jackson's eyes on him. So he turned and looked at Jackson to give him a sense of calmness.

"He seems nervous, doesn't he?" A loud voice said.

Sebastian looked back at the professor.

"I suppose it is quite shocking to see a man locked down like this. I have looked better." Said the voice.

The professor laid his head.

"It's O.K. Jackson, I have seen through a many eyes what I look like in this moronic steel contraption. It doesn't bother me anymore." Said the voice.

Jackson looked at Sebastian and said; "Man, what are we doing in here?"

Sebastian just looked at him and said; "Wait calm down. You always want to stay calm."

"Ahh, man! This is some kinda trick! What the fuck are we doing here?" Jackson said angrily.

"Wow, he's an angry one. Isn't he? You might want to do him a favor and teach him that if he wishes to continue to be around any of my off spring. He might want to conceal certain things about himself better. Especially, if he's considering attempting to remain in the shadow of my little ones."

"Yeah, I'll do that thank you." Answered Sebastian.

Fee up with this Jackson walked angrily towards the professor and something picked him up and throw him across the room. Sebastian runs over to the wall to catch Jackson as he slides down.

"Vo Comp Deactivate!" Yelled Sebastian and a loud digitized bong was heard.

Jackson landed on Sebastian and the two men were slammed to the steel floor. Jackson gets to his knees and crawls to the wall were he sits with his back against it. Sebastian continued to lay with his back on the steel floor as he stared at the ceiling.

Sebastian got to his feet and looked down at Jackson and asked. "Are you O.K.?"

He then walked over to the professor and said; "Well, it's good to see that you haven't lost your touch."

The professor seemed to look away from him.

Sebastian started to pace back and forth in front of the professor. He wanted to wait until he was good and calm before he began talking again. He knew the professor's abilities all too well and he wasn't going to make any mistakes. The elaborate security system was designed to not only hold the professor's abnormal physical strength, but also his supernatural abilities as well. Even after all these years the Federal Agencies, the Military and top Scientific Specialists from almost every community around the world still can't figure out a way to insure his control. Through trial and error, several victims have paved the way in blood for the creation and the perfection of the security system in this room.

Sebastian walked over to Jackson and said; "Don't say a word and try and think clean thoughts from now on."

Sebastian then started walking back towards the professor saying; "O.K. professor, let's chat. Vo Comp Activate."

The loud digitized bong sounded again.

"Your favorite transsexual pet gecko looking iguana, is out of control again." Said Sebastian.

The professor was quiet. Sebastian thought that was unusual, in the past he's been all too happy to hear about the occasional success of some weirdo who stumbled onto a way to ritualistically kill and leave not a trace. These cases usually can't be profiled by the usual profilers. Not a lot of them have the stomach for the rawest source of some the world's most hellish nightmares. Nightmares that originated since before the dark ages only to awaken and make history again and again. Every unimaginable nightmare comes true.

"Professor I didn't hear you. Hey Charity, is the professor's Vocal Computer System on line?" Sebastian asked.

A sweet voice filled the room saying; "The professor's Vo Comp System is Activated."

"Thank you." Said Sebastian.

"You're welcome Agent." Answered Charity.

"Well professor, there's nothing wrong with the System. So what's the problem?" Sebastian asked.

The professor was still quiet. Not uttering a word, he still continued to look away from Sebastian.

"Wait. Don't tell me that you're trying to be loyal? That's a joke." Said Sebastian as he started walking away.

"Loyal! Loyal to the very one who betrayed my research! I want it dead!" Screamed the Professor.

"Now, what do you want to do about it." Sebastian said.

"Agent, normally I would be overjoyed to assist you in your endeavor to catch my former partner. But I find myself too busy to lend you a hand with this task." Said the Professor.

"O.K. professor. I understand." Said Sebastian.

"Please forgive me. I know that you are disappointed, but I know that you're quite capable of handling him. Just use those special qualities that you know I know that you possess and I'm sure you'll do famously. Now, go on bright boy and take care that you don't get your light turned out." Said the professor.

"Vo Comp Deactivate." Sebastian yelled, as he left the steel room he heard the loud digitized bong for the last time.

The two men exited the building after retrieving their weapons. Sebastian drove to a well known cliff and started staring out at the sea. He was deep in thought, so deep that he didn't notice Danny sitting on the other side of the cliff. Jackson saw him and went over to him.

"Hey, Danny. What are you doing out here?" Asked Jackson.

"I'm just thinking." Answered Danny.

Jackson looked back at Sebastian staring out at the ocean. The two had the same facial expression. The same intense look of determination as they sat mentally working out a puzzle in their heads that only they themselves could see. After what Jackson had been through, he thought that it would be a welcomed change to sit beside Danny and try and make some sense of what he had just experienced.

CHAPTER 24

"Gustavo, would you like a roll?" Asked Danny.

"Yes please." He answered.

"Mr. Lesko?" Asked Danny.

"Jackson?" Asked Danny.

Lillian looked down at the opposite end of the table. Sebastian was sitting and staring at his glass of wine. It was obvious that he was deep in thought. She decided not to say anything. Back home before they split, she remembered how Sebastian would sit at the dinner table and just brooded over something. In the past she used to always try and get him to open up and share what he was thinking. He would always tell her that was not a good ideal. Things like that should never be discussed with the human tongue. But still she couldn't believe it. Sebastian was sitting at her table. After all this time, after all the hell in the past, there he was sitting at the dining room table.

Sebastian sensed this and looked up at her. Lillian quickly looked away and said; "If anyone's missing anything please say so."

Sebastian started thinking that she was always the perfect host. Back in St. Louis, Missouri she would have people over for dinner. Both important and just run of the mill, she always made sure that everyone was comfortable. By the end of the evening everyone always left under the good feeling of having a great dining experience. He tried looking away as feelings of great pain started to creep back into his soul. A feeling that until now, over the years he had managed to get under control. In the past it almost got him killed.

"What happened?" Asked Jackson.

"What do you mean?" Asked Sebastian

"How did I wind up on the ceiling?" Asked Jackson.

Sebastian took a deep breath and asked; "Have you ever interviewed a psychotic killer?"

"Yeah, but I've never had something like that happen to me before." Said Jackson.

"You should be happy that's all that happened. No one knows how he does anything. They keep trying new things, but it only bores him." Said Sebastian.

"Man, one minute I was there and the next I was air born." Laughed Jackson as he continued to get a handle on what happened.

"Well that's usually how things like that happen. Just all of a sudden and before you know it. It's all over." Said Sebastian.

"Just like that, huh?" Asked Jackson as he shook his head in disbelief.

"Usually people don't know enough about what they're dealing with. However some stumble onto something accidentally. Now, there are times, in some cases where something simply chooses a victim and that's what the both of them were doing." Said Sebastian.

"Grant was supposed to be dead, all these years. How is it that he's still alive?" Asked Jackson.

"You mean, you can recognize him even though he was wearing those metal rings?" Asked Sebastian.

"Back some twenty years ago, I was a member of one of several local tactical teams that responded to the University the day those kidnapped children were rescued. I saw him carried out and he looked dead to me." Said Jackson.

Sebastian, looked at Jackson and said; "You were there huh?"

"Yep." Answered Jackson as he nodded.

"Wait a minute. You mean, professor Grant is still alive?" Asked Helen.

Neither one answered. A hush fell over the entire table. She continued on to say; "Oh, come on gentlemen! I distinctly heard you say that he's alive!"

Still they wouldn't respond. Sebastian just shoved a fork full of pasta into his mouth, but Jackson looked at her and asked; "Excuse me, but who are you?"

"I'm Helen Saunders." She answered.

"The reporter?" Asked Jackson.

"You've read my work?" Asked, Helen with a smile.

"No, but I did see your missing persons pieces that my department put out." Answered Jackson.

A feeling of muteness feel upon Helen, she was suddenly left with nothing to say. Jackson went on to asked; "Now when are you going to let someone know that you're not missing or do you intend to keep it a secret?"

"What did he mean by take care not to get your light turned out?" Asked Jackson.

"The professor usually talks in riddles. Those who have high security access to him always spend an hour or two listening to him and then take several months trying to figure out what he says." Answered Sebastian.

"How was it that he's able to look at me and talk with all that hardware on him?" Asked Jackson.

"The professor's been altered. Now my guess is that whatever he didn't already do to himself, his partner must have changed him." Said Sebastian.

"The man looked right at me and put me on the ceiling! Man, you got to tell me how he does it?!" Asked Jackson.

Sebastian could see that Jackson was both afraid and excited by the events he witnessed. These are usually the first signs of a person's high susceptibility to being seduced by forbidden things. He decided to give him a little more information.

"You know Jackson, no one knows what the professor gave up to achieve his success. There must have been a series of events that led up to his unyielding motivation to leave an already established position of being a successful and well respected, noted professor of Ancient Mythological Science. Only to settle for what he's become now. Which as you saw was a powerful, raving, psychotic and a sociopathic lunatic. Who, once the day of reckoning comes, will as the good book says burn forever in the fires of a tormenting hell. Along with the rest of his bodies.

Jackson understood that Sebastian was cautioning him, he laughed and said; "Man, you don't have to worry about me. My Grandmother was the wife of a Southern Baptist Preacher. There ain't nothing the professor or anybody in this world or the next can tell me that whatever they got in exchange for their soul was worth it. There's nothing that's going to make me miss out on that day to be counted on the right hand of the, Man."

Sebastian and everyone laughed as he said. "Well you had me nervous, for a moment."

After having himself a good laugh, Sebastian took another sip from his wine glass and said; "Yeah, a lot of the times curiosity is usually just how it starts. But to answer your question. Through trial and error the Professor's room has been designed especially for him. In other words most serials have a favorite weapon. They use it time and time again, over and over. It's usually something that they take pride in like a gun, a knife and even a car. They keep these things in good condition.

Now with the professor you're still dealing with a serial. An unusual serial, but still none the less a serial. Whose favorite weapon is his supernatural abilities. He's not like any other serial. You can't just take him away from him, so the only way to disarm him is to try and limit his range or use.

Before the authorities caught on, there was research materials and lab equipment in the Professor's room. Every time they got wise or even just close enough to understanding the professor's abilities. The professor would either manipulate them like puppets or just kill them immediately in some horrible way.

The research on the professor got to be so bloody that even with high tech security measures. He was still able to more than just effectively kill at will, whenever he wanted. So with the unified efforts of most of the Scientific Communities from around the world, they started effectively restricting his abilities in almost every way. They still don't know the true depth of his actual abilities. So they continue researching him again and again every day.

As near as I can tell a lot of it comes down to the basic information that's already listed in the Bible. You know, roughly said. If you speak evil or think evil, then you've already committed evil sins. So, the metal bands slow him down. In the center they're made with a lead core." Said Sebastian.

"So, does the lead work?" Asked Uncle Aaron.

"Well yes, that and the fact that the two steel bands, his x and everything else in the room is blessed repeatedly." Answered Sebastian.

"Now, who is his partner? Do you know where to find him?" Asked Jackson.

"No, but I wish I did. See the professor won't say how he altered himself. So they don't know if he's still communicating with his partner or not." Said Sebastian.

"Who's his partner?" Jackson asked again.

At first Sebastian hesitated to answer, then he said. "I don't know it's name."

"What do you mean, it?" Said Jackson, Helen, Uncle Aaron and Mr. Lesko all at the same time.

"Look, the professor's partner. It's not a who, it's a what." Answered Sebastian.

There it goes the silence that he wanted to avoid. But now it was too late. Sebastian thought to himself that they're all in one way or another involved and they have a right to know.

Sebastian said; "There are several ways the professor could have found a way into his abilities, but I know that he was trained. No human taught him. I don't care how much he learned from one continent to another. He was spoon fed his knowledge. The professor's partner is a demon."

"So that's what that was in the shower? A demon?" Asked Lillian.

"Wait, you guys saw a demon? Asked Jackson.

"Yeah." Answered Helen.

"When?" Asked Jackson.

"Last night, in his hotel room it tried to kill us." Answered Helen.

Looking at Lillian, Sebastian became detached from the whole conversation. As they all engaged in loud conversation, he started to reflect once again on the past. A blur of historical shouting matches rushed back to him. He closed his eyes and took another sip from the wine glass. He started thinking, I shouldn't be here. I should be out hunting the one who loves to hunt us.

"Man, is there anything else you want to tell me or at least want me to know?" Asked Jackson.

"Well, over the centuries there has been much written about different rules regarding the supernatural. Those who are successful, research every stitch of known and unknown knowledge all over the world. And in most occasions even that doesn't actually give them the abilities that they're dreaming of." Answered Sebastian.

"And what does that mean in layman's terms?" Asked Jackson.

"O.K., some say that the rules are those inhabitants who exist on another dimensional plain aren't able to cross over. Some say that for every rule there is an exception and in this case, I'm afraid there's no difference. Now those on the other side do cause trouble, but there are some who are on this side of reality. They double the hell that mankind goes through. In our case I think that's what we're dealing with. The professor's abilities are far too advanced to be self taught. I think he was someone's pupil. Someone's star pupil. Now the only question is did he find his teacher or did he bring his teacher over the line? And now that he's locked up, the teacher is out of control." Answered Sebastian.

"But, you spoke like you saw it and now that I think of it. You gave him a description." Said Jackson.

Sebastian paused for a moment and said. "Look Jackson, you ought to know as well as anyone else, about the biblical story of Satan and his fallen angels. After being defeated in heaven, they now walk the face of the earth to gather souls till judgment day. I remember someone once said that the greatest deception ever perpetrated over the centuries is when Satan convinced the world that he didn't exist. So, who knows what he looks like? It could be anyone or anything."

"But, you called it a gecko looking iguana. So you must have seen it." Said Jackson.

"I've seen it." Said Danny.

Once again, all was quiet and after a moment or two Lillian asked. "What do you mean that you've seen it?"

"In a dream I had yesterday." Answered Danny.

"What did it want?" Asked Lillian.

"It kept wanting me to open the men's room door at Madelyn's Food and Gas Mart." Answered Danny.

"The door that we found you in front of the night of the murders?" Asked Jackson.

Danny nodded yes as Uncle Aaron and Mr. Lesko asked at the same time. "What did it look like?"

"It was blackish blue, with two sets of fangs, claws, red eyes and hair too." Answered Danny.

"You mean the eyes and the hair were both red? Asked Uncle Aaron. Danny nodded yes.

"Now what's that all about?" Asked Jackson.

"Every person has a door within. A door that can be opened, which allows them to travel into your body and take over your soul. Usually they use whatever trick they can to get you to let them in. Even with all of the abilities, it all still comes down to free will. You have to choose to let in them into your soul" Answered Sebastian.

"It sounded like Darla and I thought it was her, but that was before I saw it." Answered Danny.

"This was all in your dream?" Asked his mother.

Yes Danny nodded, but he felt bad. Normally he didn't want to admit any of his awful dreams to anyone ever and now that his mother knew he felt even worse.

Danny watched as she got up from the table and looked at Sebastian and said; "Excuse me, but can I see you in the next room for a moment?"

A silent table stared at Sebastian as he rose up from his seat. He took a moment before embarking upon his journey to Death Valley and finished off a large glass of wine that he'd been sipping on for the last hour.

Lillian was in the kitchen pacing back and forth. Sebastian walked in and said. "Yes Maam?"

"Ohh, don't you, yes Maam me! This has your style all over it!" Said Lillian.

"But, Dear, whatever do you mean?" Asked Sebastian.

"O! Dear, whatever do I mean! Well let me tell ya, Hon!" Answered Lillian as she walked up to him on fire.

"This has your signature all over it! So, don't try and deny it one little bit!" Said Lillian.

"And what signature is that, Babe?" Asked Sebastian.

"Admit to me. That for the same reason you didn't let me in your hotel room. Is also the same reason you made me leave St. Louis, Missouri?" Asked Lillian.

Sebastian didn't comment. Instead he was quiet and stone faced.

Lillian said. "I want to hear you admit it, just for once."

Sebastian said; "Lillian, why bring all this up now? What's it going to prove?"

"I'm sorry, but I thought you loved me." Answered Lillian.

Sebastian could see that she was hurting. Still hurting after all these years with a pain that was tormenting her to no end. He couldn't give her the life that she'd always wanted with him. The life that she truly deserved and what's worse is he knew it.

"I'm sorry, but I can't do this right now." Answered Sebastian. He turned to walk away and stopped just short of the kitchen door.

"That's O.K., Sebastian. I know that you're a busy man." Lillian said as she began to stir the sauce.

She started to crumble and stopped. She tried to hold it, but it was even too much for her to control. With all the pain in her shattered heart she fought hard and struggled to steady herself, but it was too late. With her back to the kitchen door, she started screaming silently. The pain was insatiable, as the tears filled her tightly closed eyes; she uncontrollably drew in a breath of air but unwillingly released it in yet another silent scream. She was lost and that's when she felt it, his embrace from behind, softly at first then tightly. Oh, so tightly. She threw the spoon down and turned to see if it was really him and Sebastian held her tightly to him again. With Lillian's face buried deep in his chest, she finally released it. That muffled sound of torment that she's been holding on to for far far too long.

CHAPTER 25

Little Tommy is taking a bath, his grandmother is washing his hair as he plays with his toys. Tommy Asked; "Grandmother, do we go to the zoo tomorrow?"

"Maybe, we'll have to see if it's going to be a nice sunny day or not." Answered Grandmother.

Grandmother Venetis finishes with little Tommy's bath, but she knows that he likes to continue his bathing experience so he can play with his toys. So she said; "O.K. Honey. You go ahead a play with your toys and I'll be back in a moment. O.K.?"

She leaves the boy and goes to check on Mr. Venetis and finds him asleep in his favorite chair just like always. She pulls a blanket upon him a little higher and kisses him on the forehead. Now she starts back down the hall to get Little Tommy out of the tub. When she reaches the bathroom she finds the door closed. As she takes the handle and opens the door there is a red waterfall in the center of the tub. She sees Little Tommy deep in the center struggling to scream. She lets out a scream and rushes to Little Tommy's rescue. The stream separated and washed her out of the room and she landed on the floor in the hallway, the bathroom door slammed shut. She got to her feet screaming at the top of her voice. Mr. Veneits appeared as if out of nowhere and held her in one arm and told her to go and call the police. Mr. Venetis tried the door handle, but it was locked. He took the shotgun that he brought with him and the handle. The door slowly rolled open and suddenly all was quiet. Mr. Venetis walked in and their entire bathroom was covered in blood. He looked into the tub and found Little Tommy's toys.

"But, why did you send Danny and I away? Asked Lillian.

"Because I know the day will come when I may not come home. I felt it was better to spare you and Danny now than have you both hurt later." Answered Sebastian.

"You know that's just like you to make the decision for him and I." Said Lillian.

"I did what I thought was best." Answered Sebastian

"Oh, bull shit! You should have at least asked me! Damn it, Sebastian! Why can't you level with me! I mean, did I treat you badly?! Well, did I?! I mean, even after all this time, I never even sold you into slavery for damn food stamps or child support! I don't think that I've ever asked you for very much, so, why can't you ever just level with me?!" Yelled Lillian.

"About what?!" Yelled Sebastian.

"Well for starters why didn't you tell me about those abnormal abilities? It would have helped when it came to understanding things better with our son." Said Lillian.

"Lillian, you did a great job with Danny." Said Sebastian.

"How do you know, Sebastian? I mean really, how did you know that I wouldn't screw it up? I mean, even though I made it this far without you, I'm still not through yet. How did you know?" Said Lillian.

"Simple, you're an extraordinary woman and that's your nature. You can't help, but be the exceptional women I married." Said Sebastian.

Lillian, stunned by his remark, found herself without anything to say. Back at the dining room table everyone was engaged in a heated card game.

"Now look, it was Colonel Mustered in the study with a Converse Hi top leather Air force One." Said Danny.

Jackson laughed and said; "Man, I'd like to see you make that one stick."

Mr. Lesko cleared his throat and said. "Gentlemen and Lady, I would think that my colleague is correct in his assessment of the investigation at hand, but alas, I'm afraid that in this case the young Lad has undoubtedly missed his mark. It was one of the women in the bedroom with a lawyer."

As Helen frowned and the men chuckled, Gustavo said; "Boy, what game are you playing? Cause it ain't the one that we're playing."

There was a knock at the door and Danny went to answer it. He looked through the peep hole and didn't see anything. He stood back for a moment and thought to himself that was strange. Maybe some kids were playing, but it's nowhere near Halloween. Behind him the carpet started to grow in the center of living room. As it rose the furniture around it began to topple over. Lamps and other glass fixtures shattered as they hit the floor. Danny turns to see what's going on and he is face to face with a figure covered in carpet. It wraps the carpet around him and spins. Danny is slammed to the hardwood floor as the carpet continues to wrap itself around him he struggles. He starts to yell out for help, he struggles but it covers his mouth. Once it had Danny completely wrapped up, the doorbell starts ringing faster over and over repeatedly. Wondering what was taking Danny so long; Uncle Aaron goes into the living room. He sees Danny struggling to get free of the carpet.

Uncle Aaron starts laughing as he stoops down beside him saying; "O.K. Dan. I haven't seen you do this since you were small."

The carpet flips up into a standing position. The shock of seeing this sight left Uncle Aaron frozen. He stood up and said; "Hey, how'd you do that?"

The carpet started to descend into the center of the floor. As the carpet made its way down into the floor. Danny poked his head out of the carpet and said; "Help me! It's not me and I can't get out!"

Uncle Aaron grabbed hold of the carpet with a bear grip. Tighter and tighter he pulled, but the carpet continued to disappear into the floor.

"I can't breathe! It's so tight!" Said Danny.

"Danny hold on! Help! I need some help in here!" Screamed Uncle Aaron.

As each person entered the room and saw what was happening, they immediately rushed to Uncle Aaron's side and each took hold of the carpet. The carpet disappeared into the floor right in front of their eyes.

"Shit!" Said Sebastian.

Lillian burst into tears and looking at the floor and back at Sebastian said; "Bring him back! Bring my baby back!"

The doorbell stopped ringing. Gustavo opened it and said. "Sebastian, I think it's for you."

Standing in the doorway was a dark figure wrapped in a black coat. It was impossible to see its face due to the brim of the large hat that it wore.

"He got Little Tommy too?" Asked Sebastian.

"Yes." Answered Tommy as he raised the brim of his hat, revealing his nightmarish appearance.

"Where do I gotta go?" Asked Sebastian.

"We have to go back to where it all began for us. Back to where the Professor first opened its door." Answered Tommy.

"The place of madness!" Answered Sebastian.

"I'm afraid that's correct." Said Tommy.

Sebastian stood up and walked out of the house and headed to his rental car. He popped the trunk using the key alarm. He pulled his weapon from his shoulder harness to check his ammunitions.

Jackson joined him and said; "What else do we need?"

"I can't ask you to go any further with me Jackson. It's been fun but I gotta run." Said Sebastian.

"Well that's not what I asked you." Replied Jackson.

"O.K., Well if you have a stealth missile you might want to bring it along." Answered Sebastian.

"Why, is it that big?" Asked Jackson.

"I don't know. It never really lets you see what it looks like. But when it revealed itself to Daniel I figured that it wanted him badly. So, badly that I'd better stick around and change its mind." Answered Sebastian.

"And when were you going to let the rest of us in on this revelation?" Asked Lillian.

"Well, like I said, I figured that it wanted him badly. I never said that I was sure." Replied Sebastian.

"Where are we going?" Asked Jackson, as they both opened the door and got in.

"The old Moore's estate on Zev." Answered Sebastian.

The car tore away from the curb and as they turned out of sight,

Lillian started walking back and forth. She looked at Helen and said. "Well?"

Helen smiled and nodded yes.

Mr. Lesko, Uncle Aaron and Gustavo gave each other a look after which. Gustavo said; "Now, ladies."

Chapter 26

Uncle Aaron and the ladies arrive at the old Moore's estate. They sit and wait for a moment. Mr. Lesko and his father arrive then they all meet in front of the car.

"What is this place?" Mr. Lesko asked.

"Well, back some years ago, there was this family by the name of Moore. They were rich and famous. Anyway they had a son and his name was Robert Moore. The family was deep into antiquities and ancient artifacts such as things from rare books to even an Egyptian scepter." Said Helen.

"O.K., but what happened? The place looks like the Addams family wouldn't live here." Said Uncle Aaron.

"Well, little Bobby had a friend that he met at camp. A friend that he brought home and continued his relationship with. The two boy spent a lot of time together in that house. Now, I've got a theory do you want to hear it?" Asked Helen.

Gustavo said; "Go ahead."

"All anyone knows is that little Bobby's friend's name was Teddy. I think that it was the professor." Answered Helen.

"Why?" Asked Mr. Lesko.

"Well the Professor's full name is Theodore Hurston Grant. I believe he was little Bobby's friend Teddy and together they started playing around with something that later let the professor's demon out. If the two of them didn't let it out, I believe that it most likely gave the professor his first experience with things that possessed power." Answered Helen.

"What happened to the family?" Asked Gustavo.

"The Moore's kept everything in a vault like basement. One night, while the parents slept, the two boys were in the vault playing. Something happened that night that killed both parents in their sleep and drove Little Bobby mad, so mad that he ran off that cliff and fell to his death." Answered Helen.

"How do you know all of this?" Asked Uncle Aaron.

"Because it was also in the information that Clorrissa's internet contact gave her." Replied Helen.

As Helen went back to the car to look for a flash light, Mr. Lesko and Lillian started looking at the Moore's mansion. There was a figure in the upstairs window. It looked like a little boy. Lillian and Mr. Lesko stared at him and waved at him.

Lillian walked closer to the mansion and said; "Hey, what are you doing here? You shouldn't be in there it's an abandoned building."

"Who are you talking to?" Said Helen as she and Uncle Aaron walked up beside her.

Mr. Lesko and Lillian both looked at her and said; "The little kid in the window."

Gustavo asked; "What kid?"

They all looked up at the window and there was no one there.

Helen asked; "Where are they?"

"Shine your light up there." Said Lillian.

Helen did and there was no one there. All they could see were broken windows and paint peeling off the ceiling. They all looked at each other and Lillian took a deep breath as she started up the mansion's stairs.

Lillian stopped for a moment and said; "You all don't have to come with me. I mean, I appreciate that you came this far, but I can understand if you want to turn back."

"I've got something to say." Said Gustavo.

"O.K." Replied Lillian.

"If you're going to continue to stop every few seconds and engage these little inspirational chats, I suggest that you get to the rear of the line." Said Gustavo.

"O.K." Said Lillian.

Standing in front of the huge front door of the mansion Mr. Lesko tried the handle. He turned and turned the handle, but the door would not open.

"Well, the door is locked. I guess we should all go home." Said Mr. Lesko.

Gustavo walked around him and took a look at the door saying; "It looks like the entire lock is rusted and the door is swollen shut."

Standing on the front porch in the dark of night, they started to discuss other ways to get in, until the sound of a large eerie scream over took them. They all turned and looked at the door as it slowly opened. Gustavo slapped his chest and took off his over coat. Everyone looked at him with astonishment. He was equipped with two leather ammo straps that crisscrossed his short, but stout body, he also had six pistols, two combat Bowies, an Uzi, a Samurai Katana sword which was strapped to his back and a backpack full of goodies as well. He was loaded for bear and ready for a war and he knew it.

"Dad!" Yelled Mr. Lesko in a quiet whisper.

"Yes, son." Answered Gustavo.

"What the hell is this?" Asked Mr. Lesko.

"Sherries Bartholomew Lesko. You are my son and I love you, but for now shut up and come along and we will discuss this later." Said Gustavo and then he walked into the door of the mansion.

"Yes Dad." Replied Mr. Lesko.

As they stood in the center of the great hall of the mansion, it's old moldy stale smell filled the air. It had all the ear marks of the most luxurious rich homes that you'd see featured in most old black and white movies, except it only had a few pieces of old tattered furniture and it was all covered in dirt, leaves, cobwebs and trash.

"Well do we split up or do we stick together?" Said Uncle Aaron.

"I personally don't care." Said Gustavo.

Lillian said; "I'm going up stairs to see where that little boy went to and yes, I already know that he may not be there." Said Lillian as she started up the main stairs.

Uncle Aaron followed behind her and with that so did everyone else. Once they all reached the top of the stairs, Lillian turned right and continued down the hall. All the doors of the hallway were opened except for one. Lillian went over to it and took the handle into her hand. She stopped for a moment, just to look behind her hoping that her brother or any of the crew was still with her. They were at the other end of the hallway congregating. She took a deep breath and reached for the handle again. The door knob turned all by itself and the door opened slowly. She could see that the window was open and air was blowing in. She figured that with the with window being open it must have also snatched the door open. She started to step into the room when something grabbed her on the shoulder from behind. She jumped and looked to see who it was.

"Will, you stop trying to get ahead of the rest of the group!" Said Uncle Aaron.

Lillian looked at her brother and in a loud whisper said; "You just scared the hell out of me!"

"Stop foolin around and don't walk off by yourself anymore." Said Uncle Aaron.

"O.K. O.K." Answered Lillian.

They walked back towards the group. She could hear small footsteps behind them. She stopped and turned quickly to look, but there was nothing there. Lillian continued walking with her brother. She could still hear the sound of little footsteps. The group was all together once again.

"Look this is a big place and we need to split up." Said Helen.

"She said it not me." Replied Lillian.

"Well, let's not forget that Jackson and Sebastian are supposed to be here, somewhere." Said Mr. Lesko.

"Where do you think they are?" Asked Lillian.

"Well, the vault is in the basement. Like I said it's probably where everything started." Answered Helen.

The group all agreed and started heading towards the basement. The doors were all spread out like a maze. As they started to look around Lillian, Gustavo, and Helen got lost from Uncle Aaron and Mr. Lesko.

"God, were are we?" Said Mr. Lesko.

"I just hope that we can get everybody out, O.K." Said Uncle Aaron.

The two continued down the pitch black hallway, with Mr. Lesko leading the way. Several halls away the others aren't having any better luck. With Lillian leading the way the three of them searched ahead. Gustavo found what seemed to be a study area.

"I wonder where the others are." Said Lillian.

"Hell, they're probably already with Sebastian." Said Lillian.

The two stood talking as Helen shined her flashlight on a large bookcase, while Gustavo searched for a hidden door.

"So it looks like you want him back, hum?" Asked Helen.

Lillian didn't answer.

"O.K. So don't answer me." Said Helen.

"Look Helen I gotta give it to you. You do know a lot of things, but you don't know me or my life." Replied Lillian.

"Oh, you want to bet?" Helen said boldly.

Lillian looked over at her and said; "Just drop it."

"You are the extraordinary woman who married Sebastian." Helen said as she smiled.

Lillian laughed as she shook her head.

"And yes is the answer to your next question. You guys were a little loud." Laughed Helen.

"It's been a long time, since we were together. We just had a lot to cover, that's all." Lillian said with a smirk on her face.

"So like I said, you want him back huh?" Asked Helen.

"I never lost him to begin with." Replied Lillian.

"Hey, how long has it been, since you and Danny left St. Louis, Missouri?" Asked Helen.

Lillian started to stare at the moonlight that illuminated the room. She looked up at Gustavo as he started to climb the old bookcase. She looked at Helen and said. "It was a lifetime."

Lillian walked over to the bookcase and looked up at Gustavo again and said. "Gustavo are you alright?"

He didn't answer at first, but when he finally reached the top shelf he took a deep breath and said; "No, no. I'm fine."

Gustavo took out a small hammer from his backpack and started to peck away at the wall. He had a feeling that there was an opening on the other side. After he had chipped away enough of the wall, he took out his flashlight and peered inside. He could see a passage with stairs that led down.

"Hey, I see steps that lead down. So there's got to be a way to open the bookcase." Said Gustavo.

Lillian took over shining the light on the bookcase so that Gustavo could watch his footing during the climb down. Helen started looking for the secret that would unlock the passage way. She started looking on the opposite side of the room. Once Gustavo was safely down she and Lillian joined in on the search. Lillian started looking on another side of the room. She could feel something watching her. Lillian turned and flashed her light on Gustavo and Helen, just to make sure that they were still there. After all Mr. Lesko and her brother were already missing and she didn't want to suddenly lose track of them as well.

"Hey." A voice whispered.

Lillian turned to see if any of the others were trying to get her attention, but they were both busy looking. She thought to herself that it must be her imagination. She continued searching again.

"Hey. Lillian." A little voice called out to her again.

Lillian stopped and looked in the direction of the voice. There he was again, the little boy that she had seen in the window from outside. He was peeping at her from the entranceway of the adjoining room. At first he would only show his head, but then he stepped out from behind the wall and started walking across to the other side of the entranceway. She looked to see if the others were seeing this as well, but they were unaware of what was taking place.

"Hey, Lillian." The little voice called out to her again. And when she looked again all she could see was his face waiting for her. Lillian walked over to him and as he looked up at her. She could finally see him clearly for the first time. He was dressed in a white shirt covered with a red sweater and blue pants.

She stooped down beside him and whispered. "Do you live here?"

He nodded yes.

"Are you alright?" Asked Lillian.

He nodded yes again.

"Is this your home?" Asked Lillian.

And for the third time the boy nodded yes.

He turned and pointed at a book on the shelf. It stood there by itself.

"Lillian." Said Helen.

Lillian turned and found that during her brief conversation with the little boy, Helen and Gustavo heard her talking and came to see if she was alright.

"Yes." Lillian replied.

"Who are you talking to?" Asked Helen.

"This little boy." Answered Lillian.

When Lillian turned her head back to look at the little boy again he was not there. She stood and said; "Well he was just here a moment ago."

"What did he say?" Asked Helen.

"He didn't say anything. It was what he did." Said Lillian.

She stooped back down and reached for the book. At first it wouldn't move so she tried to push it. Suddenly it started moving on its own and slid to the right of the shelf.

Gustavo heard a sound from the bookcase itself and said; "Hey, I think that did it."

CHAPTER 27

They went behind the bookcase and saw that it was opened on the side. Gustavo pulled it open the rest of the way and the three of them went inside. The stairs were narrow and the walls were filled with years of cobwebs. The two women stuck closely to Gustavo as he cleared the way of the occasional giant sized spiders, rodents and what have you. It seemed like they were walking down to hell instead of just the basement. From out of nowhere a gust of wind blew past them. It seemed to go down the stairwell in the direction that they were headed.

"That's strange." Said Gustavo.

"What?" Lillian asked.

"The air should've been traveling up and not down" Answered Gustavo.

"What if someone opened the bookcase or what if it wasn't closed?" Asked Helen.

"Doesn't matter, it still should have been traveling up and not down." Answered Gustavo.

As the stairwell opened wider, they started to see a light. Gustavo stopped.

After a moment or two Lillian asked; "What's going on?"

Gustavo said; "Wait here."

Gustavo went down ahead of them; it was difficult to see where he went because the stairwell started to spiral.

"Come here." He said.

And the two women went on to see what was going on. As they reached him they saw someone lying on the steps.

"Oh, no it's Jackson." Said Lillian as she kneeled down beside him.

He was unconscious and his clothing was all ripped off of him. Lillian started shining her flashlight down the rest of the stairwell. The others knew she was already worried about Danny and now she was adding Sebastian to her list.

"Now, this doesn't mean anything." Said Helen.

"Yeah, Sebastian seemed to be the type of man who could take care of himself." Said Gustavo.

Lillian sprang to her feet and said. "I need one of you to stay here with him."

"Wait, you can't just walk down those stairs by yourself." Said Helen.

"Why, can't I?" Asked Lillian.

"Well for starters. It's already obvious that it's dangerous down there. Maybe we should take Jackson to get some help and come back with more people." Said Helen.

"O.K. you're right. He needs help. Pick him up and take him to the hospital and I'll go on by myself." Lillian said.

Lillian continued down the stairs, she froze dead in her steps. It was a large spacious temple like clearing, complete with standing torches that illuminated every corner of the chamber. She stood stunned in the entrance way and started looking around the large room. It was cold and even though it had more than enough torches, she still could see pitch black shadows all around her.

As Lillian continued on her way into the chamber, Helen and Gustavo reached the entrance carrying Jackson. They watched as Lillian walked across the floor and when she reached the center of the room a figure wrapped in a monk like hooded robe appeared at the opposite end of the room. With the burning torch in its hand it ignited a burst of flames. A roar is heard as the fire proceeded to run in one direction. It cuts Lillian off and now she is contained in what looks like a large ring of fire. The fire doesn't stop there as the flames continue to run their course. Finally a pentagram is burning in the center of the floor. The two place Jackson on the ground and run to Lillian's aid. As they start to approach, the flames turn into a wall of fire holding them back.

Inside the flames Lillian stood scared and confused. She hadn't felt this way since she heard that voice. She tried to look through the flames, hoping for a glimpse of Helen or Gustavo, but it was impossible. She turned just in time to see him at the opposite end of the flaming circle. The hooded dark figure walked through the flames unburned. The fire seemed to melt through him. As he walked towards her she tried to get away from him, but there was no place to run. She felt weak and as her knees clasped underneath her. Her body hit the ground as the heat from the fires overtook her. With her eyes shut tight she tried to handle it all.

"Well what's the matter Lillian? You're starting to disappoint me. You were always so bold before. Where's that strong young woman that I fell in love with all those years ago?" He said.

Lillian recognized its voice. It was him the demon from her past, from the hotel. Her mind racked with fear and worry. She couldn't stop thinking of Danny, Sebastian and her brother. The fear was too great, but she knew that she had to face it. She opened her eyes and found the figure in front of her. Not wanting to show any more fear as she had been taught by Sebastian, she stood up and looked at him straight.

"Now that's better." It said as a long serpent like tongue slid out of the darkened hood, wrapped around her neck and then licked her face.

"We've got to get in there!" Yelled Helen.

"Well we can't do anything about it now." Said Gustavo in a strange calm voice.

"What do you mean, we can't worry about her now!" Helen said angrily as she turned to look at Gustavo.

The room was filled with a bunch of figures wearing hooded robs. They all seemed to be at least six feet tall or better. Each one was sporting his own battle ax or sword.

With his sword in one hand and his Uzi in the other, Gustavo went to work thinning out the herd. At one point it looked like they had him when he ran out of ammo. They rushed him and piled themselves upon him, but he resorted to small arms fire. That is if you call a semi auto fifty caliber pistol in one hand and a forty four magnum semi auto hand gun in the other, small arms.

Helen was dragging Jackson, who was still unconscious. For someone who had pride herself on knowing everything, for once she was totally lost. They started coming from the other side. It was the direction that Helen was dragging Jackson. Helen looked over her shoulder and saw them. She screamed and threw Jackson and herself on the ground. Gustavo turned, ran, and dove over them with cannons blazing; taking out eight of them.

Across the temple chamber the vault stands and deep within is a pool filled with pitch black blood. Looking at it one would think that it were a pool of molten lava. Bubbling as it rose and fell. Lying helplessly at the base of the pool, he starts to awaken. Still, tightly wrapped in the carpet Danny's head is spinning. He looks over and sees a little boys face.

"Who are you?" Said the little boy.

"Well isn't it obvious? I'm a caterpillar." Danny said sarcastically as he struggled to get loose from the carpet.

"No you're not." Said the little boy.

"O.K. your right, I'm not a caterpillar. I'm a worm." Said Danny still angry.

"Do you ever tell the truth?" The little boy asked angrily.

Danny stopped struggling for a moment, looked at him and asked; "Hey, you work for The Soft Stone Cove Police Dept. too, huh?"

"Uh unn, I'm only a little boy. My Grandmother says that I'm too young to be a Policeman." The little boy replied with a smile.

"Well if you're gonna work for the Soft Stone Cove Police Dept. I advise you not to grow up." Said Danny and then he went back to struggling to get free.

"What are you trying to do?" The little boy asked once again with a stern face.

Danny stopped once again and looked at the little boy like he was crazy.

Back in the center of the chamber, Lillian refuses to cooperate. Slam! She is thrown around the marble floor. Each time she collides onto the marble floor her body takes on the torment and agonizing impact. She lifts her bloody head and broken jaw.

"Lillian, life would be much more pleasurable if you'd only open yourself as I have." He said.

Lillian laughed and as she struggled to get to her feet she replied. "Well ya see, I'm really hard headed. Hell you should ask my Boss."

"Well ya know I believe you're right." He started laughing as he reached up above his hood and with one hand pulled it down.

Lillian took one look at him and out of shock, paused for a moment. She dropped her head and she appeared to be crying. This delighted him. He stepped closer to sock up the pleasure of misery. This was a moment he had long been waiting on for what seems like all his life. He placed his hand underneath her chin to get a good look at her broken spirit. As he lifted her face in anticipation of her defeated look, she took a deep breath and laughed whole heartedly in his face.

"Now I know it's true." Said Lillian as she laughed even harder.

"Oh, and what might that be?" He asked.

"Sai, you really really are an incredible asshole." Said Lillian.

With one hand Sai grabbed her around the throat and lifted her off her feet as he choked her. She started to turn blue and as he watched her face it suddenly sprang a look of surprise.

"Excuse me, but would you put my wife down." Said a voice behind him.

Sai turned and looked to see who was there and when he didn't see anyone he looked back at Lillian with a strange look. The look upon his face changed from one of strange confusion to finally pain. He dropped her as a hand exploded from his chest and caught hold of her jacket. Slowly the hand lowered her to the ground and once she was back on her own two feet, the hand disappeared and Sai's body collapsed to the ground. As Sai lay dying the wall of fire dropped to a low flame.

Gustavo still holding his ground was bleeding from several different areas of his hardened anatomy. Helen and Jackson were still behind him. He had no other choice but to stand and continue fighting.

"Hey, fellas, come and get it while it's hot!" Said Sebastian.

As they started to approach both he and Lillian could see them coming in full force. She looked up at Sebastian and he could feel her eyes upon him. As they closed in on them something strange started happening, their numbers were decreasing by the moment. Finally the remaining bunch started to notice that their numbers were disappearing. They stopped and started looking around. They noticed the ground starting to move back and forth. It stopped, then Tommy and his group started to rise up out of the ground.

"Hey, what can I say. You see what happens when you tell a bunch of cannibalistic cemetery eaters, that it's a free for all you can eat buffet night at the sizzler." Sebastian said with a smile as he looked down at Lillian.

With that said, the last remaining bunch tried to run and Tommy's group took them as well.

Relieved, Lillian fell to her knees, Sebastian reached down and picked her up off the floor and as he carried her said; "Honey, I can see that you've had another hard day at the office. So why don't you go find a nice shady spot and just let me go get the kids."

He placed her on the ground near Gustavo, Helen and Jackson. She saw a mound of earth run past her and got nervous.

Sebastian smiled and said. "Hey now, just sit and play nice with the other parents and I'll be right back, O.K."

As he started to walk away he stopped, turned and said; "Gustavo, damn good job! Damn good!"

Gustavo, out of breath and dripping with blood and sweat, acknowledged him by shaking his head yes.

Sebastian and Tommy walked up to the vault door.

"How do you want to play it?" Asked Tommy while he straightens the Ray Bans that Sebastian gave him.

"Well, best way I figure it. We can blow the locks or we could just ask it to open." Replied Sebastian.

Sebastian walked up to the vault and knocked three times. "Fuck you!" was heard in the shape of thunder.

They both looked at each other and said; "O.K."

Sebastian sat down and pulled Lucille from his backpack. When he opened her, he could see by her computer screen that she was still processing Data.

Suddenly she said; "May I help you Sebastian."

"I see that you're still working on that problem for..." Said, Sebastian.

"Would you like me to hurry?" Asked Lucille.

"Yes, dear. I'm in a hurry." Answered Sebastian.

The schematic design on her monitor started to speed up in rotation and within moments a six minute timer appeared in the upper right hand corner.

"I'll set the explosives." Said Sebastian.

Sebastian ran back to the vault and started setting the explosives. He looked above him to see how high the other explosive charges had to be set and went to work on setting the ones on the bottom.

"Hey can I help?" Said Gustavo.

Sebastian turned and asked; "Are you sure?"

"Yeah, I just got some rest." Answered Gustavo as he reached into his backpack and pulled out a grappling hook complete with thick, black nylon climbing rope.

Sebastian watched Gustavo as he held a bundle of rope in one hand and started spinning the hook in the other. Gustavo threw his hook with accuracy, which landed on the head of a Gargoyle that was centered over the top of the vault. He reached into the backpack and pulled out a pair of foot claws and started climbing. Once he was in position Sebastian threw him the explosive charges and as quick as lightning he went to working on installing them.

Sebastian was done. With three minutes left on Lucille's monitor he looked up to check on Gustavo.

"How's it going?" Asked Sebastian.

"Almost there." Answered Gustavo.

"All right, we're down to less than three minutes." Said Sebastian.

Sebastian started looking at Lucille's Data. Suddenly a live link was established and he received an incoming e-mail alert. He accessed the information and once he was finished Lucille's monitor started a countdown of less than a minute.

Just as Gustavo was ready to connect the final wires linking the other eight points of the charges, he feels a tug on his rope, and when he looks up the Gargoyle is still stationary. He stops and starts to look at it more closely. The hideous head snatches him into its mouth. The claws begin to push him inside, more and more. Half out and half in like a gun slinger, Gustavo quickly draws one of his cannons from his holster. The sound of thunder is heard throughout the temple's chamber walls. Three fourths of the Gargoyle's head rains down on Sebastian and Tommy.

"And you said it would never snow in sunny Southern California." Sebastian said to Tommy, who replied by shaking his head no with a wide grin.

The first of eight explosives ignited as Gustavo repelled to the ground and ran as the rest of the charges began to blow one by one. Dust and smoke filled the air. Sebastian, Gustavo and Tommy stood, waiting for it to clear. As the thick fog started to settle, it became clear the entire twenty foot tall vault door was still standing.

"Well you guys got any more bright ideas?" Asked Helen.

"Yeah, run." Said Sebastian as he reached down and grabbed Lucille and started running.

The other three stood there confused. Suddenly, sounds of metal cracking started to give, echoed throughout the temple's chamber. All at once thousands of pounds of steel vault door started to fall. Gustavo, Tommy and Helen took off running. They ran past the place where Sebastian was now standing. The vault door hit the floor of the temple and made a deafening sound. The impact was that of an earthquake as the shock wave shook the foundation. The fog was thicker and denser now. Sebastian started walking towards the opening. He stepped upon the smoking hot vault door and proceeded to walk across it. As he neared the opening he crossed him and suddenly stopped just short of the center of the vault door. The fog encircled him while the others were cut off. Sebastian stood silent, waiting. He knew that he was not alone. As the dense fog swooped and swirled all around him he continued to pray. A face formed in the fog behind him.

"Well, well, well. If it isn't the Protocol Son and to what do I owe for the pleasure of this little visit?" It asked.

"You've been a very very bad, pet. Gecko!" Answered Sebastian.

The face disappeared from behind him and several whirls formed and began spinning all around him over and over.

"Speaking of pets, you were my favorite lab rat and now I am so pleased that you've come home." It said.

"Why didn't you take my advice?" Asked Sebastian.

"And what advice was that?" It asked.

"Why didn't you go to hell?" Asked Sebastian.

Another face formed above Sebastian as it replied; "Perhaps all I needed was your company on the long trip. A nice doll to play with during the long drive home, if you will."

"Gecko, how many times do I have to tell you? You're not my type." Answered Sebastian.

"You still don't have a sense of humor, child. And if it's the last thing I do. I will teach you that." It replied.

The dense fog started to spin around him faster and faster. A mighty gust of wind rushed him and almost knocked him over. Sebastian stood calm and quiet as he patiently waited for all this to pass. Sebastian jumped out of the way as a huge fist struck the place where he was standing. He moved again dodging its tails. Sebastian dove into the fog trying to get a fix on its location. He began throwing steel cylinders from his backpack. After several steel canisters were thrown, Sebastian was struck by its tail. The impact sent him flying through the air until his body smacked into the wall at the far side of the temple. Lillian and the others watched as Sebastian's body slid down the wall of the temple. Lillian tried to get to him, but a pair of arms held her back. Seeing Tommy and the others still in front her she turned to look and see who it was.

"You do look like you're half Gecko and half Iguana." Yelled Jackson as he hit a switch tapped to the palm of his hand.

All of the canisters ignited and a blue gas was admitted into the air. It quickly over took the thick dense fog as lightening and bolts of electricity streaked through it. It began wailing at the top of its voice as the blue mist overtook it. And the jolts of electricity tore it apart. It wailed and wailed as it fought against the pain. Suddenly there was silence and after a long pause came the sound of a huge crash. It felt and sounded like someone had dropped a tow truck in front of us.

"Maam, are you all right?!" Maam, maam, I said are you all right?!" Asked a Federal Agent who was wearing a white bio suit.

Lillian looked up and she saw several Federal Agents in white bio suits flood the temple chamber. Jackson released her arm and she turned and looked at him.

Jackson smiled as he started to explain; "Yeah, Sebastian told me to pretend that I was totally unconscious and it was hard. He said under no circumstances are you to even open your eyes and that was the hardest thing I ever had to do in my life. Then he said when the time came to it this little buzzer would go off in my hand and that would be the right time to push this button. And man I'm here to tell ya that when it did, it was just about the right damned time."

Lillian went in the direction where she saw Sebastian's body fall. As she made her way around the steel vault door to get to the other side of the temple, she could see it for the first time. It struck fear in her soul just to see it lying there, even with the Federal Agents all over it. She found the place where Sebastian fell but he wasn't there.

"Mom! Mom, here I am." Said Danny.

Lillian ran to Danny and wrapped her arms around him tightly. She burst into tears and said; "Thank you God! Thank you so much God!"

Beside Danny with tears in her eyes she noticed a little boy, she asked; "Well you must be Little Tommy?"

Little Tommy started wiping his eyes and yawning at the same time. Lillian asked; "Ahh, are you sleepy?"

Little Tommy responded by slowly shaking his head yes. Lillian picked him up and kissed him on the forehead and continued hugging them both.

"Hey we got another survivor coming out of the vault!" Yelled one of the Federal Agents.

Danny looked over and saw Dene stumbling around. He ran to her and held her tight as they slowly sank to the ground.

"Where were you?" Danny asked.

"All I know is that I was working with Darla one moment and that thing came out of the cooler. Next thing I know is that I just woke up here and found this guy untying me." Said Dene.

"It must have been Sebastian." Said Danny.

"Who's that?" Asked Dene.

"He's my Farther." Answered Danny.

Jackson standing with them said; "I'm going to look for him."

"Don't bother, I just came out of there and there are no more survivors." Said another Federal Agents.

"Wait a moment, describe the guy who untied you." Lillian said.

Dene described Sebastian and Lillian looked at Danny.

"Yeah, Dad untied me too Mom." Said Danny.

Once they all got outside the mansion, they found Uncle Aaron and Mr. Lesko standing next to all the Federal hi-tech trailers along with a horde of Federal Government Agencies. Once again they were all united and safe and the nightmares were over or they would be at least for the time being.

CHAPTER 28

Sitting in a bar restaurant in St. Louis Missouri's Central West End, he was relaxing and reading the Sunday Post Dispatch news paper.

The waitress brings him a stack of butter milk pancakes with a pile of sausage and bacon, an order of sunny side up eggs all resting on top of a mountain of hash browns with a huge sirloin porterhouse steak. He just completed reading an article about how last week Federal Agents rounded up a group of terrorist that were discovered living in a old mansion in Southern California. He smiled as he looked at the photo of Jackson, Gustavo, Mr. Lesko and Helen who reported the story. He shook his head no in amusement as he heard sounds of someone going through his newspaper at the opposite end of the table. He let the top portion of the newspaper fall. As it folded there she was, just sitting at the other end of the table, reading the sales sections.

"Oh my, God. Just look at these prices. I mean, can you believe it?" She said as she continued to turn to the next page.

He flipped the newspaper back up and as he turned the page he asked; "Are you sure you know what you're doing?"

The waitress placed another cup of coffee on the table and as she took a sip she replied. "Um hm. Well let's see. Danny and Dene are shopping and Aaron's back at our house getting ready to barbecue. Yeah, I think that's it."

He turned another page as he said; "Well, as long as you know what you're doing."

"Oh, yeah. I did forget one more thing." Said Lillian.

And after a moment of pausing he straightened his newspaper and asked; "And what might that be?"

She snatched the newspaper out of his hands and sat down on his lap and looked into his eyes and said; "I love you."

And with that she embraced him in a deep, strong, long, romantic kiss and for a moment in time the world stood still just for them as they held each other, ever so tightly. St. Louis Fire House's Engine number nine screamed past the bar. They stopped briefly to look and then turned back to each other and smiled. They both shook their heads no as they laughed and continued their slow deep kiss once again.

Later that same evening as the Polezogopoulos household slept, a little boy is walking across the ice. He is lost and alone as he travels through the extremely cold harsh land. He sees another child in the distance. She is walking aimlessly trying to find her way as well. He starts out to try and catch up to her and as he closes the distance he can see her stop and fall to the icy ground. The little boy begins to run and just as he gets within ten feet of her, he hears something move underneath the icy floor. He stops and looks at her as the beast makes the most terrifying sound. He's close enough where he can see her hysterically crying as she attempts to crawl towards him on the ice. In one instant the beast breaks through the ice and in gulped her in one bite, and with that it than disappeared back underneath the ice. What he saw and witnessed was so devastating that he fell to his knees in despair. As tears started to race down his face, he began to pray to the Lord to take him now. The beast let loose another roar and the ice began to crack underneath him once again. He could feel all hope start to slip away from him.

"Hey, what are you doing?" The little boy looks up and sees his father standing in front of him.

"I'm scared Dad." Said the little boy.

"Stand up." Said the Father.

The Father takes hold of the little boy's hand and helps him to his feet. The Father starts to brush the ice and snow off of the little boy. The beast again let loose another terrifying, roaring scream as more ice cracked underneath their feet. The little boy looked down at the bloody hole in the ice.

The memory of the little girl still fresh in his mind, the little boy said; "Dad it's down there."

Standing beside him the little boy's Father said; "Take my hand."

As the two of them stood there on the ice, for a moment, the little boy could see it swim underneath them through the ice.

"But Dad, it's down there." Said the little boy.

"Just take my hand." Said the Father.

The little boy reached and took his Father by the hand and as the two of them began walking his Father looked down at the little boy and said; "Baby, he's always been down there, so who cares and besides, he's not the scariest one here anyway."

"He's not?" The little boy asked.

The Father stopped and pointed at the little boy's heart and said. "No, this is."

With the sun high above them, the little boy took the hand of his Father once again and the two continued their walk upon the ice.

The End.

Printed in the United States
By Bookmasters